# WHERE RIVERS GO TO DIE

"The stories of Dilman Dila leap from the page and grab you by the throat with intrigue and urgent imagination. An impressive American debut!"

—Tananarive Due, American Book Award winner

"Get ready for strange truths written in pure, powerful words. Frightened and curious, hopeful and brave, the heroes of Dila's stories lead his readers through razor sharp dangers to the rewards gleaming at every one of his stories' surprising and satisfying ends. From sheer delight in the futuristic flight of Ugandan ornithopters, to sweetly nasty certainty as to the alien identity of the "savages" bedeviling clueless white colonizers, Dila delivers pleasure after pleasure to minds eager for fiction's freshest glories."

—Nisi Shawl, award-winning editor of *New Suns* and author of *Everfair*

"A book filled with spirits, monsters, resource wars, techno organic horrors, trans dimensional beings, wondrous machines, and so much more. Where Rivers Go to Die reads like literary episodes of Love, Death, and Robots meets Black Mirror, doused in African fantasy, folklore, and futurism. Dilman Dila shines here as one of the most creative storytellers of our age, weaving together an impressive set of imaginative, character driven, and reality-bending tales examining issues of everyday life, gender, spiritualism, politics, war, and exploitation through the lens of the strange, the bizarre, and the otherworldly. The genre needs more like this!"

—P. Djèlí Clark, author of *A Master of Djinn* and *Ring Shout*

"Amongst contemporary storytellers of the Afrocentric speculative, Dilman Dila's work inhabits a locus occupied by few others. Every tale thins the border between the is and the could-be: boosted by straospheric imagination while grounding you in the concerns of the contemporary African. I never pass up an opportunity to read a Dilman Dila story."

—Suyi Davies Okungbowa, author of *Son of the Storm*

"Dilman Dila deals in dualities. This collection by one of Africa's most consistent speculative fiction authors is an excellent showcase of his ability to defy genre and effortlessly blend superstition and science, fear and fascination, reality and unreality, uniqueness and universality, into wonderful, exciting stories steeped in culture. Full of immersive worldbuilding and a persistent horror sensibility rendered in sharp, efficient prose, Where Rivers Go to Die is a highly enjoyable read."

—Wole Talabi, author of *Incomplete Solutions* and editor of *Africanfuturism: An Anthology.*

"Dilman Dila is a well-established figure in the African Speculative scene. His various disciplines -film-making, animation, writing etc - inform all aspects of his work holistically. Among the results are thoughtful, deep-reaching tales, constructed upon a firmament of rounded research and experiential detail. His sparse, journalistic style amplifies the strangeness of his narratives and at times his voice resembles a slightly supernatural Hemingway.'"

—Nikhil Singh, author of *Taty Went West* and *Club Ded*

# WHERE RIVERS GO TO DIE

## Dilman Dila

Cover art and design by Bizhan Khodabandeh

Rosarium Publishing
P.O. Box 544
Greenbelt, MD 20768-0544

www.rosariumpublishing.com

# ::: **Table of Contents** :::

# ::: Fragments of Canvas :::

A gust blew in through the window, chilling Inspector Winyi out of sleep. As he searched for the blanket, his phone rang. He cursed. He had turned it off at midnight. He wanted to berate his wife for switching it back on. She always warned that he would miss a very important call if he kept it off. His sweet Atim. He came fully awake when he realized she could not have done it. She was dead.

"Hello," he grumbled into the phone.

"There's a corpse in Rock Hotel," a voice said in Kiswahili. A woman. She had a familiar accent, like that of Atim, who had grown up in Mombasa. "It's in the honeymoon suite."

For several seconds Winyi could not respond. When he did, anger thundered in his voice.

"Call the station!" he said, and hung up.

His thumb moved to the power button. Only then did he notice that the phone was off, the screen blank. Had he imagined the call?

The curtains fluttered in the breeze, reminding him of Atim in her bridal gown. The cold ripped through his flesh. He frowned. They were in the middle of the dry season, and yet black clouds prowled around the moon like dogs around a bitch in heat. Were the rains coming?

He closed the wooden shutters. He found the blanket on the floor and wrapped himself. Still the chill persisted. The cold licked his bones. His teeth clattered.

The phone rang again. It was off, yet it was ringing. He rationalized the phenomenon. Though not a smart phone, he could set an alarm, switch it off, and go to sleep. At the scheduled time it would turn itself on. Maybe it had a similar function to allow incoming calls.

He checked the number flashing on the screen. His frown deepened. There were only five digits, not the proper ten. It could not be an automated call like the ones from telemarketers, those had three digits. Puzzled, he pressed the YES button.

"Go there right now," the woman said, gentle but firm. "You were chosen a hundred years ago to do this job."

She hung up. The chill vanished instantly.

For nearly a minute he kept the phone pressed to his ears, though no sound came through. He broke out in a sweat, the sheets stuck to his skin.

He tried to call her back, but a robot said, "The number you have dialed is incorrect."

He glanced at the clock. Three a.m. He called the station. Thirty minutes later, a patrol truck pulled up outside his door. He lived in the police barracks in a row of identical buildings, none of which had received paint in twenty years. The asbestos roof had cracked, and it leaked during the rainy season. The windows and doors had rotted with mold. Being in charge of the Criminal Investigations Department in the district, he had a cottage to himself with a spare bedroom. It sometimes made him feel guilty, since lower ranked officers crammed their families into extremely small tin huts.

Four uniformed officers sat in the back of the pickup, fondling AK-47s. They mumbled indecipherable greetings. None saluted. He had woken them up. He could have waited until morning. It might even have been a prank. He got into the cabin. The driver, also uniformed, grumbled in response to his greeting.

The hotel was a colonial palace. When Winyi arrived, its staff had not yet cleaned the garden of debris from a wedding feast. Garbage floated in the swimming pool. Under the three party tents, overturned chairs gathered dew. Bottles, used paper plates, cake crumbs , and leftover food littered the lawn. It took thirty minutes to awaken the night manager, who escorted them up the stairs to the honeymoon suite.

A woman in a bathrobe opened the door, scowling, her eyes red. She was in her mid-twenties with elaborately braided hair. Atim had been an advocate for African hairstyles. She would have been proud of this bride's choice.

"Sorry to bother you, madam," the night manager said. "But the police—" he could not continue for several seconds. "They want to search the room."

"Why?" she barked. Her breath stank of alcohol.

Winyi wanted to apologize for disturbing her wedding night. She did not look like she had a corpse in the room. It might have been a prank call after all.

"Where's your husband?" he said.

She sighed. "Asleep," she said. "Can't this wait until morning?"

"We only want to make sure there is no dead body in there."

"Dead body?"

"Apart from your husband, is anyone else in there?"

"No! Of course not!"

"We have to search. It'll only take a minute."

"No!"

She started to close the door. He put his weight on it. She glowered at him for several seconds. He kept a smile on his face. Finally, she stepped aside to let him in.

"Only you," she said. "No one else."

"Okay," he said.

Inside, the smell of sex stung Winyi's nose. He had not made love since Atim died three years ago. Like most honeymoon suites, this one had a red theme. The rug on the floor, the bulb, the bed spreads, they were all red. The white bridal gown lay discarded on the carpet beside the groom's suit. A champagne bottle and two wine glasses lay on the table. Empty. The man was on the bed, seemingly asleep, the sheet pulled up to his neck.

Winyi checked the bathroom. No corpse. He looked under the bed and inside the closet. Nothing. He turned back to the man on the bed and touched his neck, searching for a pulse in the carotid artery. Nothing.

"He is dead," he said to the bride, who stood, arms akimbo, at the other side of the bed.

"You are mad," she said.

She climbed onto the bed and shook her husband.

"Honey, wake up," she said. She shook him so hard for nearly two minutes, slapping him, as she descended into tears. "Honey, wake up," she cried. "You are not dead. Wake up."

The other officers walked in. They cuffed her and gently dragged her out.

Winyi searched for a visible cause of death. He pulled the sheet off the corpse. On the chest he found a wedding ring and a piece of canvas. He went down on his knees to examine the ring. He was no expert in jewelry, but he thought it was pure gold, with "Okot and Aceng Forever" etched on the inside. He checked the man's fingers. No ring.

Why did the killer put it on his chest? Was it a case of jilted love?

Maybe the bride found out he was cheating on her and staged a perfect revenge. But then there was that phone call. Was the caller the other woman? What did she mean when she said that Winyi had been chosen a hundred years ago to do the job? What job?

The body bore no visible signs of the cause of death. No bleeding. No bruises. No stab wounds. No bullet holes. No strangulation marks. No vomit from poison. Nothing.

Winyi tried to pick up the ring. It was glued to the canvas, and the canvas glued to his skin. Only then did it occur to him that the canvas was also an important clue. About half the size of A4 paper, it was worn, shapeless, a pale brown color. He ripped it off the corpse. It left a raw red patch on the body. Bits of skin and hair stuck to it.

"The clock," an officer said. "Look at the clock, afande."

It said ten thirty, yet the time was a quarter past four. The second hand ticked dutifully, though the minute and hour hands were dead. The sound of its ticking now echoed like the heartbeat of a demon. Atim had died at ten thirty in the morning.

Winyi took it off the wall. It was a replica of a mosque. On the back was the drawing of a small boat with a lateen sail, a dhow, under it was a line in Arabic.

"That does not belong here," the manager said.

:::

The next day Winyi questioned the bride. She claimed not to know of any affairs her husband had. They were a happy couple. Nothing strange had happened during the wedding. They partied with their families, then retreated to the honeymoon suite and made love and fell asleep. She woke up when Winyi knocked on the door.

"He died of happiness," the pathologist said when Winyi went to the hospital after talking to the bride. "I'll still run more tests, but I won't find anything. His heart simply stopped beating because of happiness."

Establishing the cause of death would be the first step to unraveling the mystery. It had to be a murder. The call in the night, the strange clock, the ring, and the canvas, they all confirmed it as an unnatural death.

Winyi wished he had the resources of the police forces in Europe and America. They could comb a crime scene to pick up clues invisible to the eye. He could not even dust the room for fingerprints. He had to rely on his intellect. Sometimes he got lucky and had witnesses. Sometimes the analyses of Dr. Othieno, the pathologist, helped him. Yet the doctor also worked with limited resources. Maybe if they sent the body to Mulago, the National Referral Hospital, they might find answers. The relatives of the dead would have to foot the bill.

"Happiness?" Winyi said.

"Yep," Dr. Othieno said. "Some hearts can't handle it."

Winyi turned all his hopes on the call. The mobile phone company gave him a list of all the calls he had received the previous day. There were only two numbers. One was from his mother, asking for money, and the other from his brother, also asking for money. It was the only reason his relatives ever talked to him. The log did not show the call that had tipped him off.

"She bewitched him," the groom's mother said. "We paid them a lot of money for bride price, and he had a lot of property. Now she thinks she can kill him and take over everything? She's a fool. She won't get even a coin!"

They refused to send the body to Mulago, preferring instead to consult a shaman. Winyi rubbished their allegations. He needed something logical to take to court. The only thing that pointed to foul play was the call, but since he could not verify it, he had no evidence that a murder took place. He had to close the case hardly two days after the murder.

He took the clock, the ring, and the canvas to his home. When the groom's family tried to reclaim the ring, he told them it was still an exhibit. He did not tell them he had closed the case. He wanted to retire, to get away from all things that reminded him of Atim, and start a new life. This ring could give him the means. He had no use for the canvas and wanted to throw it away, but it was stuck to the ring. He could not separate them. He tried using a knife, tried burning it, but it was as if the canvas was also made of gold.

He feared his mind was cracking, that he could no longer discern reality from fantasy. Was the canvas really indestructible, or was he only imagining that it could not be separated from the ring? And that strange clock, was it stuck at the time of Atim's death?

Had he really gotten a phantom call? But if not, how had he known about the groom?

Had the caller really sounded like Atim?

For three years he had tried to get over her death, with some success. Now the strange case reminded him of his own honeymoon. The reveries did not last. Images of her death gave him nightmares. He had not been there when it happened, but witness testimonies played over and over in his head until he could see the ice cream hawker on the pavement handing her a cone, the truck speeding out of control, her blood mixed with ice cream on the tarmac. She had been four months pregnant with their first child.

He could not hold it anymore. He had to see her just one more time.

He had locked away their memorabilia in a suitcase that he kept under his bed. He pulled it out. A film of dust coated the metallic surface, hiding its green color, its red flower design. It had a padlock. He had thrown away the key to beat the temptation of opening it, so he used a hammer to break it open.

A photograph lay on top of the pile. She took it three days before she died to show off her young pregnancy. After a decade of trying to conceive, the swelling had made her life a paradise. It was the last photo she ever took, sitting on a fake rock in a studio, a painted waterfall in the background, her smile exposing the gap between her front teeth ... Something was wrong. Her skin. It used to be the color of black coffee. Now it was several shades lighter, a reddish brown, like fried chicken. Her hair too had grown longer, the braids falling down to her breasts.

Dizziness swept over him. Was memory playing a trick or had the photograph changed? Other photos also showed her as he remembered. Maybe someone had replaced one of her photos with that of a woman who looked like her.

The next day he did not go to work. He went to the bar and got drunk. He staggered back home at midday, pulled the suitcase out from under the bed, doused the contents with paraffin, and set it all ablaze.

Maybe it is better that I don't recall what she looked like, he thought, as he watched the flames licking her face into oblivion. Maybe it's a sign that I am ready to move on.

The fire went out quickly. Everything in the case turned to ash, apart from that photo. It survived intact. He struck another match, but he blacked out before he could torch it.

He woke up the next morning to find it hanging in the living room in a gold-colored frame with a design eerily similar to that of the clock, which also hung on the wall, still stuck at 10:30. He rationalized that his maid had paid an artisan to design the frame and that she had hung it up. Nothing else made sense.

But when she brought him breakfast she saw the photo, and said, "That's wonderful. It's not good to forget people you loved."

The rest of the day passed in a haze. He did not understand what people said to him. He could not speak, could not see clearly. He felt a chill, even though the sun turned the town into a blazing hell. Atim ran wild in his head, tormenting him with images of resurrection. He was afraid to go to the living room. The clock and the photo were on the wall in there, the ring and canvas locked in a drawer in the entertainment unit. He could not go there. To get into or out of the house, he used the back door through the kitchen.

He could not sleep.

Had Atim called from the other side to tell him about the dead groom? But why? What did the clues mean? The clock, the ring, the canvas, what did they have to do with her? Was the clock stuck at the hour of Atim's death? If he turned the hands to read the correct time, what would happen? Would it take him back to the past to be with her or forward to the future? What would he find in the future?

He drained a bottle of whiskey to help him sleep.

:::

The next Saturday, exactly one week after the first case, she called again. As before, a freak storm gathered in the middle of the dry season. Lightning flared, illuminating the room with ghastly blue flashes. Thunder blasted. A chill blew in through the window. He shivered. The dead phone pierced his eardrums. Déjà vu filled him with dread. He sat up on the bed, every muscle stiff. He did not want to answer, yet curiosity prompted him to press the YES button.

"Hello, Inspector," she said.

"You," he said, not knowing what else to say. He pressed the phone against his ears. It felt like a brick of ice.

"How have you been?" she said.

The coastal accent. Atim's accent. Yet it could not be Atim. She did not sound like this. What then had she sounded like? He had forgotten what she looked like. How then could he be sure this was not her voice?

"Atim?" he said. His throat was inflamed, preventing more words from spurting out.

She giggled. "There's another corpse," she said. "The same room."

He swallowed saliva, but it cut his throat as if he were drinking shards of ice.

"Why are you telling me?" he croaked.

"You were chosen."

"For what?"

"You'll soon know."

"Atim was not a murderer."

"In the eyes of the ancestors, sacrifice is not murder."

The phone went silent. Her voice echoed in his ears for nearly a minute. He looked at the screen. It was blank. Off. The window was open, the curtains swayed in the breeze. The storm clouds dissolved into white cotton, allowing the moon to shine. The beams fell onto his bed like love letters.

He turned on the phone, wondering whether to call the station. Before he could make up his mind, it rang. It was the hotel's night manager.

Inspector Winyi reached the honeymoon suite fifteen minutes later. The groom's corpse lay supine on the bed. On its chest sat a wedding ring, a silver piece with three stones that Winyi thought were diamonds on another scrap of canvas. He looked for another clock on the wall. Nothing. The bride cowered on a sofa far away from the bed.

"He just died," she said, her voice a dry whisper. "We

were making love, and he just rolled off as though he was going to sleep."

Sacrifice is not murder, but sacrifice for what? Was Atim the killer? Why did she kill these two men? What do they have in common?

Maybe there was nothing spiritual in their deaths. Maybe they both shared an ex-girlfriend and the jilted woman was on a rampage killing all the men who had dumped her, waiting for their wedding nights before she strikes. Maybe she used a poison that left no trace. Maybe she used a special gadget to call his phone. It could all have had a simple explanation. Nothing supernatural. He had to pursue a logical chain of thought. He could not blame his dead wife.

He had to reopen the first case.

Serial killer. He had heard that term but never encountered such a criminal. It had to be a serial killer because of the signature, the groom's ring on a canvas glued to the victim's chest.

"Did you put this on his chest?" he asked the bride.

Her lips moved, but no words came out, so she simply shook her head.

"Then how did it end up on his chest? Where did that canvas come from?"

She could only shake her head and cry.

:::

The second death in the same suite hit the front pages of the national dailies. Fortunately, Winyi had not yet sold the golden ring and the clock. He returned them to the evidence room. The media exposure put pressure on the police, and this in turn gave him a lot more resources. He sent the body to Mulago, but the top pathologists in the country failed to find the cause of death. He sent the clock, the pieces of canvas, and the rings to Makerere University. He got a report within three days. The rings belonged to the victims. So nothing came out of it.

The clock and pieces of canvas created more questions. They were over a hundred years old. The Arabic inscriptions on the clock translated into, "Only Allah can stop time." The fragments of canvas came from an oil painting. Somebody had scraped the paint off and then ripped the canvas to pieces. It was made of hemp and looked ordinary. The lab could not explain why it was stuck to the ring, or why it was indestructible.

This scared Winyi. The two pieces did not make up the entire painting. Did that mean more would turn up on the chests of dead grooms? How many?

The telephone calls provided him with the only means to solve the case. After the second death, he got them every night. He talked for hours with the caller, his dead wife, he was now convinced, but the next morning he could not remember the conversation. He felt it had something to do with love and marriage. He felt she was seducing him. When he began to expect her calls, to miss her during the day, to wish she did not call only in the night, he knew that he was falling in love with the ghost.

It had to stop.

He discussed it with Headquarters, and they sent a team of technicians. However, when they set up their equipment in his bedroom on Thursday night after the second death, she did not call. He feared that he had indeed imagined the whole thing, that he was truly losing his mind. That he was talking to an imaginary person through imaginary phone calls.

But how could he explain the tips?

The technicians did not despair. They had played the waiting game before, sitting idle for days waiting for their wiretaps to pick up information. They stayed up the whole night and slept through the day and waited again the next night in vain until Saturday. The day of weddings.

No couple booked into Rock Hotel's honeymoon suite. The police considered it a crime scene, and the management kept it closed. Even if it were to be open, no one would have dared book it. With it empty, Winyi hoped nobody would die that night.

Still he did not get any sleep. He sat on his bed, waiting, reading a novel. He wondered if his choice was appropriate. Amos Tutuola's *The Palm Wine Drinkard*. After the first four chapters he resorted to a newspaper.

At three a.m., when the temperatures dropped and a chill blew into the room, when clouds swept across the sky and blanketed the moon, when lightning erupted and thunder blasted, he knew she was coming.

He did not know how much he had missed her until that moment. His heart pounded the way it had trembled the first time he met Atim. She had figured out his shyness and took control of the dating until he became bold enough to propose. This night caller was indeed Atim. She was rebuilding that scenario, taking control of the seduction, pulling him into a trap.

He did not want the technicians to hear this call. The phone was on a table set up beside the bed. It was attached to a laptop computer, which would record the conversation, and a SteengRay, a box-shaped device that would enable them to trace the caller. Winyi suspected the device was a pirated product from China, the original was called "StingRay". The two technicians were in the living room, watching TV. He had not told them about the signs of her coming. He had only a few seconds to make a decision, to unplug the phone from their gadgets and press YES the moment it rang. Before he could make up his mind, they walked in and puzzled over the abrupt change in the weather. Just then the phone started to ring.

They sat on stools, wore headphones, and began the trace. He pressed YES.

"I'm disappointed," she said.

"Why?" he said.

"You want other people to listen to our conversations," she said.

On the computer screen red dots appeared all over a

map of the country. The tracking machine needed only a few seconds to pinpoint her location.

"I'm a police officer," he said slowly, playing for time so the machine could track her. A thousand lights blinked on the screen. The techies cursed in whispers for the Chinese machine was confused, picking up signals in places where there were no telephone towers. "You seem to know something about these deaths. Why don't you tell me the truth?"

"There's another dead groom in Elgon Resort."

In Mbale town, twenty-eight kilometers away.

"How do you know?"

She hung up. The techies gaped at the screen. The blinking dots went out. The SteengRay was supposed to keep her in its grips, even if she was not making a call or sending an SMS, as long as her phone was on. Maybe she had turned it off.

"Did you at least record her voice?" Winyi asked.

They played back a WAV file. It had his voice, but in place of hers, there was only static.

"Chinese junk," one of them jeered.

:::

The next day when he got to Mbale, the local police had not entered the room. They were afraid. A rumor was spreading that it was a ghost, Winyi's dead wife. In the honeymoon suite a mganga dressed in bark cloth performed rituals with a dead chicken. The corpse lay on the bed, another piece of canvas on its chest. A silver ring gleamed in the sun. Again there was no clock.

"Why did you kill him?" someone said behind him.

He turned to see a woman in her mid-thirties in a night dress walking into the room. Before he could reply her fist slammed into his nose. He fell backwards, shocked more than hurt. She charged at him, but the shaman grabbed her and dragged her out.

"Why did you kill him?" she yelled. "You witch!"

He returned to Tororo thirty minutes later with the clues in a polythene bag. He retrieved the first two sets of ring and canvas out of the evidence room and laid them on his office desk. If they were from the same painting, he thought, maybe he could fit them together like pieces of a jigsaw. Maybe it would tell him something. It took him only a few minutes to figure out where each piece in the jigsaw fit. They merged perfectly. He could not see the seams.

Then the rings melted into a thick red liquid. Blood? It indeed was the odor of blood. It dissolved into the canvas, which changed from pale brown to azure. Now the smell of oil hit his nose. He closed his eyes for several minutes, holding his breath, but when he opened them again he still could not see the rings and the canvas remained blue. He could still smell the paint.

He touched it. Paint smudged his finger tip.

After nearly fifteen minutes of staring at the canvas in shock, he got the nerve to push the three pieces apart. At once they lost the blue color and regained the age-old pale brown look. The smell of oil vanished. Blood seeped out of each and congealed into the three rings.

:::

That night, when his phone rang, he did not answer. The techies were gone, having given up the mission as futile unless they got genuine equipment. The phone screamed in his ears like a siren. He had always thought there was a rational explanation for it all. Anything was possible with technology. But not metallic rings turning into blood. Not wet paint appearing out of thin air. He had always thought she was a real person who might replace Atim, who might help him find love again. Not anymore.

She was evil, a monwor, a spirit that took the shape of a woman and lurked at the roadside like a prostitute to trap men.

The phone kept ringing.

He did not answer. It occurred to him that, without it, she could not talk to him. So if he got rid of it, he might get rid of her. He ripped out the battery and tore out the SIM card. Still it did not go silent. It vibrated in his palm like an angry bee. He buried it in a sack of flour in the kitchen. It kept ringing, but the sound did not hurt his ears anymore.

On his way back to the bed, a strange noise, like a rapid taping, erupted in the living room. He peered. Atim's picture glowed red. The wind made it shake and rattle against the wall. Her braids now flowed down to her waist.

She blinked.

He looked away, hoping it was only a trick of his exhausted mind, but when he glanced at her again, her smile widened until he could see her tongue, as red as blood. He fled.

He did not sleep that night. The temperature plunged. His skin froze. A fierce wind blew outside. Lightning exploded like the flash of an evil camera. The blast of thunder hurt him. The distant ring of the phone and the rattling of the picture bore into his skull like a saw. The torture would end if he answered the call. The cold would vanish, the noises would cease. He would find sleep. Still he refused to pick up the phone. He wrapped the blankets tighter around his body. He persevered until the first lights of dawn broke out.

:::

A few hours later, as he walked to the station, he said hello to the officers he by-passed. They looked away without responding. Some fled on seeing him. In his office he found the fragments of canvas, the rings, and the antique clock on his desk. He had put them back in the evidence room the previous day, vowing never to touch them again. Why then were they in his office? As he stood at the doorway, puzzling, he heard footsteps. He turned to see the District Police Commander approaching, waving a newspaper.

"Have you read it?" The DPC showed him the headline: "Is The Police Practicing Witchcraft?" "It says that, since you receive calls from your dead wife, you have something to do with the murders."

"This is stupidity," Winyi said.

"I know," the DPC said. "But you must go on leave to allow an investigation."

Winyi gaped at the DPC for a long moment. He wanted to protest his innocence, but he simply walked away.

"Winyi," the DPC said. Winyi stopped. "Take those things with you."

He meant the exhibits from the murder scenes: the fragments of canvas, the rings, the clock. Winyi did not want them either. Silently, he walked back home.

He lay on the bed, wondering what to do next. Sheer exhaustion knocked him out. He slept until two o'clock when the maid woke him up for lunch. As he sat up, he at once became aware of the phone on the bedside table stained in flour. He thought she had taken it out of the sack. He was about to yell at her when he looked up to see her holding a polythene bag.

"They sent these from the station," she said.

She placed it at his feet and walked out. He did not have to look to know the contents.

:::

He stuffed the clues, his phone, and Atim's picture into a bag. He hired a motorcycle boda-boda to take him five miles out of town. He then walked into a mango forest, dug a deep hole, and buried the bag.

That night at three a chill woke him. He pulled the blanket tighter around his body, but the temperature kept dropping. He wore extra clothes, but his teeth could not stop chattering. Lightning flashed in fury. Thunder made the walls shake. It wanted to kill him, he thought. He could save himself if he dug up the phone and talked to her, but he brushed away the thought. He would persevere like the previous night. When morning came she would give up, and then he would find a mganga to help him ward her off forever. Icicles formed on the window. The blanket turned into a sheet of ice. He saw his breath in the pale lights of the moon, and he heard her voice in the wind.

*You were chosen a hundred years ago.*

He could not bear it. He would freeze to death unless he answered the phone. Though it was far away, he knew it was ringing. He staggered out of the house. Wind whipped his face. There were two cars in the yard. They belonged to other officers. He chose the nearest, a Toyota Mark II, with a cracked windscreen. After several minutes of trying, he hotwired it.

He sped to the forest. The fuel gauge was nearly empty. He passed two petrol stations. They were locked up. He kept driving, praying that the gas took him all the way. It stalled about half a mile off. He completed the journey on foot. He felt warmer with each step he took.

As he unearthed the bag, the phone rang from under the ground. Desperate, he dug, afraid it would stop before he got to it. And then he would freeze to death. He dug, praying for strength. When he touched the phone, it was like finding a fire. His blood turned warm. The sheets of ice on his skin crackled, and warm sweat soaked his clothes.

"Please," he cried. "Leave me alone."

"You were chosen," she said.

"Why?" he cried. "Why me?"

"I'm your jajja," she said.

"My what?" he said, though he knew what she meant. Ancestor.

"There are four more pieces of canvas," she said. "It's a painting I made just before my ship sank. You must collect them for the picture to come alive."

The phone went silent. She was gone. The message sank in. The painting would come alive, just as Atim's photo had come to life with an evil smile. But what was in the painting?

*I'm your jajja.*

He knew a bit about ancestral spirit possession. Many shamans claimed they never chose the profession, that they were called against their will. They surrendered to the ancestors to save their lives. Once they accepted, they did good. They healed the sick, blessed crops, made businesses prosper, made rain in times of drought, they did good. This one could not be an ancestor. She was killing people. Besides, painting on canvas was not an indigenous African art. How could his ancestor have been painting on a ship that sank?

She was evil. She was a monwor. He had to stop her. He had to save the next four grooms. A mganga could help him.

Over the next days he visited seven shamans in three different districts. He did not tell them his name. He asked them to discern the purpose of his visit. They failed. They were quacks. Then he found a half-blind old woman whose face was so wrinkled that he could not figure out which lines made up her lips. Her shrine was a small circular hut, dimly lit, with the only light coming through a tiny window. Strange beads, shells, skin, and bones hung on the mud walls. Banana fiber dolls swayed on strings attached to the grass roof.

"You have trouble with a phone," she said to him.

Impressed, fingers trembling, he gave her the rings and canvas. She placed them on a flat, straw tray and pieced them together. The fragments merged. The rings melted into blood. The smell of paint hung in the air as the canvas absorbed the blood and turned blue.

"It's your grandmother," the old woman said. "From a very long time ago."

Winyi felt a tickling sensation in his spine. If it was his grandmother, why was she seducing him? Why did she want him to think she was Atim?

"What does she want?" he said.

The old woman threw bones and shells onto the incomplete painting and stared at them hard for a few minutes.

"She was taken as a slave," she said. "She married an Arab and had a child. They stoned her to death for being a witch. Many generations later, one of her daughters married a trader. She was an Arab girl. She was a painter. She convinced her husband to come to the source of the River Nile to search for a fortune. It was your jajja guiding them back home. In the desert her powers were very weak for she was far from home. But as she neared home she grew stronger for she could communicate with the source of her powers. Unfortunately, as they crossed Lake Victoria, a storm sunk their boat. She drowned at ten-thirty in the morning."

Atim had died at the same time. He looked at the ship on the back of the clock, at the inscription under it saying, "Only Allah can stop time."

"She wants to come back," the mganga added.

"She already came back," Winyi said.

"Yes, but she's trapped in the body of an Arab. She has to possess a body with her original bloodline. It's a very complicated case. That's why she needs the ritual of seven grooms."

*Sacrifice is not murder.* Bile rose to his throat. Why him? Why did she force him to become an accomplice in the murder of innocent grooms?

"Why do spirits possess people?" the old woman asked, and Winyi wondered if she had read his mind. "My father was a shaman. When he died everybody thought the spirit would fall into one of my elder brothers, but it waited twenty years until I was in university studying to be a lawyer and then it fell on me. Why?" she shrugged. "I'll never know."

"Did you kill people?" he asked.

"She's not evil," she said. "She is a very powerful spirit. She'll do a lot of good. It's sad that she needs the seven grooms, but sacrifice is not murder. She's a good spirit."

:::

On Saturday night she told him where to find the fourth ring and canvas. He jumped onto an old motorcycle, which he had bought earlier that day, and rode to Bugiri, a small town on the highway to the city. He found the lodge with little difficulty. Unlike Rock Hotel and Elgon Resort, this was a cheap, dirty hotel. Many of the window panes were broken.

A woman opened for him. The smile on her face told him that she did not know her husband was dead. He said he was an angel. She did not understand. He explained that he had come to take her husband's soul to heaven. Confused, she hurried to the bed and tried to shake him awake. Then she started to ululate. He ripped off the ring and canvas and fled before anyone could answer her screams.

He went into hiding. The woman would tell what she saw, and that would confirm his guilt. They would arrest him and throw him into jail, and then the jajja would not resurrect. She would kill him for it. He did not know why he was doing it, whether he believed the old mganga that she was a good spirit, but she had chosen him. He had to accept or die.

He cut off his beard, which he had kept for three years, and used black dye to get rid of the shades of gray in his hair. He looked ten years younger. He ditched his coats and ties for jeans and t-shirts and wore a wide-brimmed straw hat to complete the disguise. The hunt for him was nationwide with his picture splashed on the front pages, but that did not worry him. He had a new face. He moved from town to town, never spending two nights in the same place, picking very cheap hotels where the management asked no questions.

Waiting for the next victims was torture. The days seemed like years. But Saturdays eventually came, and thousands of weddings happened all over the country. He used burglar tricks to get the next two sets of rings and canvas, stealing them without awaking the brides. The seventh groom was in Sangalo Beach Resort Hotel on the shores of Lake Victoria. He had to subdue and truss up a guard before breaking into the honeymoon suite, where he found a bride still in her gown, trying to awaken her dead love. He hit her on the head, and she passed out. While the first scene had an antique clock, in the last one he found a paintbrush. He had to pry it out of the dead man's fingers.

Back in his hotel room, he put the seven fragments of canvas together. The rings melted into blood and dissolved into the canvas. The wet blue paint appeared. Was it the waters of the lake? There was nothing else on the painting, just an empty blue expanse.

He waited for it to come alive. It did not. He waited for the spirit to possess him, but nothing happened until the brush rattled. It was on a table beside the clock. It vibrated like a wingless insect trying to fly. It smeared the tablecloth with red paint. Or was it blood?

He touched it. Electricity struck him. A strange force took control of his body. Was it the spirit? He became a puppet. His hand moved fast over the canvas, leaving red smudges that materialized into elements in the picture: white clouds, a dhow with white sails, an Arabian bride on the deck. He finished the painting just as the cocks started to crow. The sun would soon rise.

Finally, the minute and hour hands of the antique clock moved until they said the right time. Five a.m. From the past to the present. Only Allah can stop time. Now the clock ticked like the heartbeat of a happy demon.

Outside, the storm that had threatened for seven weeks came down hard. In the painting the dhow rocked on the waves, its single sail swollen. The only person aboard was the bride. She looked straight at him.

The painting will come alive.

He stepped away, his mouth dry with fear. It was not an Arabian bride. It was Atim. His dead wife. Her long braids flowed in the wind. The storm swept into the painting. The waves tossed the boat. She clung to the ropes. He thought he heard her scream, whether in delight or pain, he could not tell. A whirlwind hurled her out of the painting. She ballooned into a life-sized person as she hurtled through the air. She fell on the floor with a sickening thud.

This was no spirit possession.

He sprinted for the door. She grabbed his leg. Her hands were cold and scaly, like fish. He tripped and fell, smashing his nose onto the floor. Blood spurt. She turned him around to face the ceiling and then fell on top of him, pinning him down, placing a ton of bricks on his chest. Water dripped out of her hair onto his face. Cold, freezing water.

He could not see Atim in her, though she had Atim's face. Her skin was the color he remembered, coffee black, but her eyes were like that of a doll, as though made of glass. Dead eyes without any light in them. Eyes that betrayed what she truly was, a sorceress. She had used him and had impersonated the old blind mganga to lie to him, to make him believe she was a good spirit. And in those eyes he saw what she wanted, his final purpose.

She brought her lips to his. He turned his face away. She held his cheeks in her cold, cold hands, such that he could not escape her kiss. The scales tickled him. Her lips came down again, slowly, the way Atim's had come down when she wanted to kiss him.

He started to cry. "Please don't," he croaked. "Please."

Her lips, the cold, cold lips of a fish, touched his, in a deep kiss, like that of lovers, and she sucked, and sucked, and his life flowed into her body, and her body grew warmer, as his grew colder, and colder, until he was swept away into eternal darkness.

## ::: Kifaro :::

Jamwa knew where he was the moment he woke up. The emergency room. Machines bleeped. Medics worked in near silence. He could not understand how he got there. The last memory he had was his phone ringing in the lab. Did he answer it? Who called? He sat up. The medics did not notice. They continued to work as though he were still supine. He turned to see his head on the pillow, deep cuts on his cheek and forehead, eyes closed as though in a peaceful sleep.

"He stopped breathing," a nurse said, monitoring a screen that displayed his data.

"He still has a pulse," a doctor said.

"But brain activity has increased—" The nurse pointed at an image with a million red dots flickering. "He is dreaming."

"Oh, no," the doctor said.

"Should I unplug—" the nurse began, but the doctor interrupted her.

"No!" the doctor said. "He still has a chance. Put him on the ventilator."

Another nurse fit a mask on Jamwa's face and inserted a tube through his mouth to enable him breath. His chest began to rise and fall.

"He's still dreaming," the monitor nurse said.

The doctor ignored her and focused on his torso, which she had opened up. The sight of his shattered organs sent him staggering off the bed. He watched as they tried to stop the bleeding from several mesenteric arteries. Something heavy had smashed into him. He would need a new kidney, and he would lose parts of his intestines ... if he survived.

Recent research on near-death experiences revealed that, when the spirit leaves the body and the body remains alive, the brain interprets the out of body experience as a dream that could last from a few minutes to several days. Only in a few cases did the spirit return to the body and the person recover. In order not to waste resources, the government had instructed all hospitals to unplug patients if near-death dreaming started.

Jamwa glanced at a clock on the wall. Twelve-thirty. From his wounds he must have arrived at the hospital within the hour. That meant disaster had struck while he was still in his office, but what happened? An earthquake? A terrorist bomb? And that phone call, the last thing he remembered, did it have anything to do with this? Who made the call and what had it been about? His eyes darted from one medic to another, expecting them to give up any moment and unplug him. Minutes passed. His heart continued to beat. The life support machines bleeped. The ventilator helped his chest rise and fall. His brain continued to interpret the experience as a dream. The doctor did not unplug.

A stifled cry sent him running to the waiting room. He knew that voice. His wife. Immy. She and his two girls, Lakeri and Buba, sat on a bench while a receptionist stood behind a desk. An elderly man in a striped suit and red tie stood by the outer door. They all turned to the ER door when it opened. When no one came out, Immy ran toward it to get a glimpse of her husband, but the receptionist stopped her and gently forced her back to the bench.

"I want to see him!" Immy cried.

"Who opened the door?" the monitor nurse said from the emergency room. "No one gets in!" She closed the door firmly.

Immy calmed down. Lakeri was only eight, Buba only six, but they were the strong ones. They whispered encouragement to their mother.

Things had not been good after Immy found out about the student. Acila. He never intended to have an affair, but

Acila had been irresistible. He seduced her with the promise of a job at the East African Center for Disease Control, where he worked. When he failed to secure her a position, she told Immy, and Immy started to think of divorce.

*It's okay*, Jamwa said. No sound came out of his mouth. *It's okay, it's okay.* He placed a hand on her shoulder to comfort her. She shuddered at his touch and looked up.

"Jammie," she whispered.

Lakeri grabbed her mother's cheek and forced her to look away.

"Look at me, mum," Lakeri said. "Keep your eyes on me, mum."

"I can feel him," Immy said, placing her hand on his. Only she could not touch him. So her fingers rested on her own shoulder. "I can ..."

"No, mum!" Lakeri said. "He's still alive!"

Immy let her fingers slide off her shoulder. "Of course," she said, crying again. "He's still alive." Her shoulder shuddered again. He thought this time it was to shake off the ghost, so he withdrew his hand, and her body relaxed. "I imagined it. He's alive."

As he stood watching them, he sensed somebody staring at him. He pirouetted to meet the elderly man in a striped suit with a neat white beard and eyes so white they might have belonged to a newborn baby. The wrinkles on his face, rather than speaking of old age, gave him a youthful look, almost as if they were trendy scarifications.

"Hello," the man said. "I'm Ondego."

Jamwa stepped away from him. Is this a Child of Bukuku? Is he here to guide him to the other side?

"You aren't dead," Ondego said. "Otherwise, that lovely doctor wouldn't be working so hard to save you."

Two things struck Jamwa at once. The man could read his mind, and eerily, Immy and the children could not hear him although he spoke aloud.

"They can't hear me because I don't want them to," Ondego said.

"Excuse me, sir," the receptionist said. "How can we help you?"

The man stepped closer to her. "I'm a friend of the family," he said. "How is he?"

"Please take a seat," the nurse said. "The doctor will soon let you know."

"Thank you," he said, and turned back to Jamwa. He did not sit. "Do you know who attempted to murder you?"

*Murder me?* Jamwa chuckled. *What nonsense.* But then he glanced at the ER and wondered if that explained everything. Someone wanted him dead, but who could—the thought froze and he turned to Immy. The day she found out about Acila she had confronted him with a knife. She would have stabbed him if her sister had not intervened. Now her grief seemed genuine. Was she putting up a show for the children?

"That's a thought," Ondego said. "But it won't help to question her now. Before we investigate, you must help doctors stop the bleeding."

*Eh?* Jamwa said.

"Here." Ondego pulled a sachet made of bark cloth out of his coat pocket. It contained a green powder. "Put this in your bloodstream."

*What is it?*

"Medicine. It'll keep your body alive, but you'll remain in spirit form. They won't unplug you. I made sure of that. You have to help me catch your murderer."

Questions blasted Jamwa. Who is this man and how did he make sure the doctor did not unplug him? In the end the answers did not matter. He was alive. He had a chance to be with Immy and the girls again, another chance to be a good father and a good husband. He did not want to leave them in pain. He spread out his palm, and the man gave him a pinch of the powder.

He kept his hands down, hoping no one would notice powder flying through the room. He opened the door to the ER. The medics around his body were too engrossed to notice, but the monitor nurse snapped at the receptionist.

"Who opened the door?" the monitor nurse said.

"Someone inside," the receptionist stuttered. "Not us."

"How is he?" Immy asked, hurrying to the monitor nurse.

"Please be calm," the nurse replied, closing the door. "We are doing our best."

Jamwa approached his body, careful not to touch any medic, and released the powder into his bloodstream.

"What was that?" a nurse said.

"What?" the doctor replied.

"Something green ..." As she spoke, a greenish paste appeared on the punctured arteries and the bleeding stopped.

"Jesus," the doctor said.

Jamwa walked out. This time the monitor nurse, who joined the other medics in staring at the paste, did not react when the door opened by itself. Jamwa saw understanding dawn on her face.

Ondego walked out into the corridor, and Jamwa followed, giving his family only a brief glance. If he lingered, he would touch Immy or the girls, and that would scare them. They walked out of the emergency ward to the parking lot.

"We'll start from the crime scene," Ondego said, getting into a blue Land Cruiser.

They sped through the sleepy streets of Tororo and turned off the highway five miles outside town onto a new tarmac road that led to the gates of the East African Center for Disease Control. There were ten guards rather than the usual four. Two searched the car for weapons. One in the security booth placed Ondego's ID in a scanner to verify its authenticity and log his visit.

"What brings you here?" the guard asked.

"I'm Jamwa's lawyer," Ondego said.

The guard seemed unsure but pressed a button, and the gates slid open.

*Who are you?* Jamwa asked as they sped through a driveway in a forest full of birds and small animals.

"I hunt for kifaros."

Jamwa frowned and looked out of the window at a squirrel racing up a tree. That could only mean he was some kind of mganga. Kifaros were evil spirits. Assassins. Had someone sent one to kill him?

"I found a luong'jogi in your car," Ondego said.

To send a kifaro a mulogo gives a luong'jogi charm to a murderer, who plants it in a place the target frequents—at home, at the office desk, in a car—and the charm guides the assassin to the target. Was this hunter able to detect these charms? *But after he found one in my car,* Jamwa thought, *why did he not stop the kifaro?*

"If I had not intervened," Ondego said, "you'd be dead."

*You used me as bait,* Jamwa said. *If you removed the charm from my car, the kifaro would not have hit me.*

"I saved your life," Ondego said.

Jamwa wanted to retort, to rage, to question why he stopped the doctor from unplugging him. *What does he want with my spirit?* But Ondego was not to blame. Someone had sent the kifaro after him, someone close to him.

Kifaros were never used on random strangers. The victim was always someone the murderer knew—a neighbor, a friend, a relative, a business partner, a workmate. Someone very close. Immy? He did not want to think about it. A workmate? But his position as a researcher was not competitive. His uncles? His father had passed away the previous year, bequeathing him a hundred acres of land. Three of his uncles pressured him to sell. The eldest was a Pentecostal pastor. Could he consult a mulogo for the services of a kifaro? The other two were farmers, and they openly worshipped ancestral spirits. They might have known which mulogo had kifaros. Were they so evil that they would kill their nephew over land?

Maybe it was Acila. She had a strong motive for revenge. He slept with her but did not give her the job.

*Did you catch it?*

"No. It's an evolved kifaro. I couldn't detect it."

The building he had worked in for the last five years developing a vaccine for HIV was a three-story structure of glass and steel. There were police officers all over the front yard where visitors parked. Ondego drove to the staff parking lot behind the building. He stopped at the barricade. In the booth, instead of the usual guard, was a cop.

"You can't go in there," the officer said. "It's a crime scene."

"Open," Ondego said in a soft whisper, and the woman lifted the barricade.

*Mind control*, Jamwa thought, frowning at Ondego. Was that how he stopped the doctor from unplugging him?

Ondego did not respond.

There were five staff cars and two police vans in the yard. At the far end yellow tape encircled Jamwa's Jeep. The driver's door was crumpled. Glass scintillated on the ground amid pools of blood. A wrecked motorcycle lay beside the car. It apparently had rammed him against the Jeep. Crime scene detectives went through the debris. Was the charm still in the car? Would they find it?

"No," Ondego said. "The charm evolved as well. It looks like fast food trash. Chicken feet wrapped in napkins instead of banana leaves; a chicken head with bits of your hair on the comb stuck on a plastic fork and chicken entrails wrapped around a chopstick instead of the usual coffee tree stick."

*Walkie-talkie and shoelaces*, Jamwa thought, a dish that once was only for the poor who could not afford prime chicken parts. Then East Africa united, and the ensuing economic boom catapulted large sections of the poor into a strong working class. They did not let go of chicken heads, feet, and intestines, which became a national favorite.

A plain-clothed detective was talking to Jamwa's workmate, Karama, who had taken off his lab coat. Jamwa had never seen him without a lab coat. Dark patches showed under his armpits. He kept passing a hanky over his face.

The detective, in a gray coat with no tie, had a notebook in his palm as he chewed on a pen. He was not writing.

Ondego stopped the car close to them. They did not notice.

"I donno," Karama was saying. "He said 'hello,' then listened, then dropped the phone, and fled. Maybe the caller told him there was a bomb under his desk. Then we heard the crash and came out to find him dying by his car and the strange bike."

"And the biker? Did you see him?"

"No."

"Whose bike is it?"

"I don't know."

"But it's in the staff parking lot. It must belong to one of you."

"I've never seen it before. We all drive cars."

The detective snapped his book closed and spat out the pen.

"You are hiding something," he said. "How did that bike get in here? How come two sets of guards never noticed it?"

"I don't know," Kamara said. "I don't know."

"Liars!" the detective cursed.

*That call*, Jamwa thought, *it does not make sense.* A kifaro always left no doubt that the death was the work of a supernatural force, if not an act of nature. But here he got a call whose details he could not remember, and it lured him to the parking lot where a motorcycle rammed into him. These marked it as the work of an ordinary murderer, not that of a supernatural assassin.

"A mulogo has created a new type of kifaro," Ondego said. "Their hits look like ordinary murders. Police often puzzle over confusing clues like this phone call and the motorcycle, but they are always convinced the killer is human."

Jamwa had never thought about how kifaros came to be. Spirits often served the community for good. Upon his death a mganga might use his spirit to make irizi to help people seeking knowledge or to help students pass exams. In the same way successful business people end up in charms to help business people and successful farmers help farmers. But kifaros ... Did walogo, the dark side of waganga, use murderers?

"Every spirit is a good spirit until a mulogo turns it," Ondego said. "My job is to find kifaros and rehabilitate them, but a mulogo has made a new kind that I can't detect."

"Trace the call!" Karama was shouting at the detective "It has something to do with his death! Trace it instead of harassing us!"

"There was no phone call!" the detective said.

"I heard it ring," Karama said. "I saw him answer it! I saw him panic at whatever the caller said, and I saw him run out! Trace it!"

"We checked his call log! We checked with Banana Telecom! We checked!"

"I don't believe this," Karama said.

"Just tell me who killed him—"

"Find the caller!" Karama shouted.

"Maybe you'll give better answers from the station," the detective said.

He nodded at two uniformed officers, who handcuffed Karama and shoved him into the van. Jamwa saw four other workmates in the van, handcuffed.

"I'll check your phone," Ondego said.

He got out of the car and walked to the detective. They talked for a few minutes, then the detective went to the second police van and pulled a plastic bag out of the back. It had Jamwa's phone. Ondego scrolled through the log, then handed it back to the cop.

"They can't see the number," he said when he got back into the Land Cruiser. "The mulogo keeps it hidden. You can't remember anything because the moment you answered the phone the kifaro took control of your mind."

Fifteen minutes later, they were at the offices of Banana

Telecom in Bazaar Street. Ondego left Jamwa in the car and went in, returning hardly ten minutes later with a piece of paper.

"The number is registered to this person," he said, handing Jamwa the paper. "Does it ring a bell?"

Jamwa studied the name. Omondi Joseph. It did not mean anything. The paper listed a home address in Kasoli. They sped to it. The suburb had been a slum until the East African government built free housing for the residents. The buildings were shaped like huts, cylindrical with conical roofs, and painted in vivid colors. Children played football in front of Omondi's block. Many window panes were broken, and garbage overflowed from a bin. They went through a lounge littered with junk furniture, then up a murky staircase to the fourth floor through a corridor with charcoal graffiti. Children laughed behind Omondi's door as a TV played at full volume. Ondego knocked.

"Turn that down!" a woman shouted from inside. "Burayan! Turn it down!"

The laughter continued, but the TV's volume went down. The door opened, and a woman smiled at Ondego.

"Children!" she said. "They are too much. How can I help you?"

"I'm looking for Omondi," Ondego said. "Joseph Omondi."

"He's at the garage," she said.

"Can I ask you a few questions?" Ondego said. "I'm his friend. I just need to know a few things."

The woman looked unsure, but Jamwa thought Ondego got into her head to make her obey. She stepped aside to let him in.

*Search the house*, Ondego said to Jamwa. He did not speak aloud.

*For what?* Jamwa said.

*Anything*, Ondego said. *We need to know who this Omondi man is.*

"Get off the sofa," the woman told the children. The

sofa was worn out, faded from purple to a pale blue. The three children, aged between six and ten, slid to the floor, their eyes glued on a sixty-inch flat-screen TV, which was out of place amidst the musty, broken furniture. They were watching a sci-fi comedy about a group of East African astronauts stranded on Mars.

Ondego and the woman sat on the sofa. Jamwa searched the house. Framed family photos beamed on the walls beside a large crucifix with neon lights and a digital calendar of Sacred Heart Cathedral. The apartment had a tiny kitchen, a rolled-up mattress in a corner, and a pile of half-washed dishes in the sink. The floor was wet. The bathroom was too clean. The children's bedroom revealed nothing but a mess of clothes and broken toys. The parents' bedroom was neat. He looked through the drawers and the closets but found nothing. Just as he was about to give up, he saw a hole in the ceiling.

He found a torch and climbed on the dressing mirror to pull himself into the ceiling, where he found a metallic box. It had a padlock. He went back down into the bedroom and searched until he found a bunch of keys. He tried them one at a time until the padlock snapped open. The box contained a newspaper article and a family photo. The article, dated seven years back, was about a man called Amanya Hope, found dead in what looked like ritual sacrifice in Mbarara town, over six hours away by bus. The writing on the back of the photo identified the people in it. Amanya Hope, his wife, and their five children. Jamwa had to look closely to confirm that Amanya Hope was Omondi Joseph, even though Omondi had darker skin and a beard.

Jamwa went back down. The children still made noise in front of the TV. Ondego looked up on sensing Jamwa, and Jamwa waved the article and the photo. Ondego then excused himself, and the woman saw him to the door. Jamwa was afraid that the children or the woman would notice the newspaper and photo floating in the air; but the children were engrossed by the TV, and Ondego distracted the woman until Jamwa was out of the apartment.

"Ha," Ondego said, on reading the article. "Very clever. It lives like a mortal and even has a wife and children. No wonder I couldn't find him."

*It's him?* Jamwa said.

"This kind makes my work a nightmare," Ondego said. "Let's go to the garage."

*But how can a dead person have a wife and children?*

"He controlled her mind to get her to marry him," Ondego said as they hurried down the stairs. "He controlled other men to impregnate her without her knowledge."

The garage was a metal shack under a mango tree with broken cars, dead motorcycles, and scrap metal scattered about. Four men in grease-stained clothes sat on the ground playing a board game, Ludo. The smell of roasting pork and beef wafted from the nearby market while the sizzle of a river in the valley below provided a background hum. Weaver birds made a racket in the mango forest that choked the banks. As the Land Cruiser snaked into the yard, two men abandoned the game and rushed to it.

"Boss," one said. "I'm the best mechanic. What's the problem?"

"I'm looking for Omondi," Ondego said.

"That one is lousy," the mechanic said. "Hire me."

"He's fixing that lorry," the other mechanic said, pointing to a green truck, and both returned to the game.

Jamwa and Ondego got out of the car and walked to Omondi, whose feet peeped from under the lorry. He was banging something, but stopped abruptly.

"He notices us," Ondego said.

Omondi slid out, a spanner in his hand. His eyes lit up on seeing Jamwa.

"You ..." he began, but the words got stuck in his throat. He scrambled to his feet like a student after the headmaster caught him doing something illegal. He was lanky with a scraggly beard. He dropped the spanner, reached into his pockets, and pulled out a cigarette. His hands trembled.

"Who sent you?" Ondego said.

Omondi tried to respond but could only make a gurgling sound. His voice trembled worse than his hands. He could not strike the match. He again looked at Jamwa and spat out the unlit cigarette.

"Do you know me?" Ondego said.

For a response Omondi ran. Ondego pointed a finger at him. A rope shot out of the finger and caught Omondi's leg, sending him crashing to the ground. Omondi threw a fireball, hitting Ondego in the tummy, and Ondego yelped in pain. The rope unwound itself and twitched on the ground like a beheaded snake. The mechanics backed away in terror. Free again, Omondi ran hard.

"Don't let him get away!" Ondego said. "Get him!"

Jamwa ran after Omondi, who was racing down the valley to the bridge. Omondi looked over his shoulder, saw what was chasing him, and dived into the river. Jamwa followed him in. Omondi kept close to the riverbed, swimming at an incredible speed, as though he were a speedboat, but Jamwa overtook him and grabbed his legs. Omondi threw a fireball at Jamwa, but Jamwa did not feel any pain. It was just as though a hot breath had swept over him.

"You!" Omondi said, throwing another fireball, and when it did not hurt Jamwa, the fight went out of him. He collapsed onto the riverbed in surrender. Jamwa dragged him to the banks. Women washing clothes farther down the stream paused to stare.

*Who sent you?* Jamwa asked.

"Your uncle," the kifaro said. "Mabaga."

The youngest of the three who had pressured him to sell the land and the poorest, but with the largest family. He would not inherit the land unless his elder brothers passed away, which meant that he intended to kill them all.

"The fire doesn't hurt you," Omondi said.

*My body is still alive*, Jamwa said.

"He forced me to do it," Omondi said, his voice weak.

Ondego was running on the water surface. He scared the women, who fled into the mango forest. A rope again shot out of his finger and, like a boa constrictor, wound itself on Omondi, tying him up in a few seconds.

"I tried to stop," Omondi said. "He hurts me if I refuse."

Ondego knelt beside him. "I'll protect you," Ondego said. "I'm a won'jok. Just tell me who your master is."

Omondi's face relaxed into a smile when he heard that name, won'jok, the father of spirits. Some communities worshipped them as gods. Ondego must have been a powerful and famous shaman who lived a hundred years ago. But why was he in flesh and blood? Jamwa wondered.

"Jjungo," Omondi said. "His shrine is—"

"I know Jjungo," Ondego said. "I thought he was a good one."

"Please," Omondi said. "Help me."

Ondego sprinkled the green powder on Omondi while chanting in a strange language. Omondi's spirit left the body, which degenerated into putrid flesh. He gave Ondego and Jamwa a smile and walked off into the mango forest.

Ondego got into the minds of every human nearby to make them forget what they had seen and stop the mechanics from forming a lynch mob. The rotting corpse remained on the banks. The police later wrote it off as an unidentified drowned man. Jamwa felt sorry for Omondi's wife, who would never know what happened to her husband, but it was for the better. How would she have reacted if she discovered he was a walking dead creature, a spiritual assassin?

They sped to Jjungo's shrine in Kisoko sub-county. They drove over sandy roads and had to make the last five hundred meters on foot for there was only a path cutting through a thick bush.

"He's expecting us," Ondego said. "He is powerful and might hurt me, but you'll match him for you are still alive."

Jamwa had expected a mud hut with a grass thatched roof as the shrine, not a cylindrical brick building with a neon sign on the roof blinking Jjungo's name. The door and windows were closed. Red light flickered through the cracks on the wooden shutters. Ondego pointed at a window, and a flame consumed it within a few seconds. They peeked in. Much of the décor was common in shrines, charms, bead artwork, and masks on the walls. Figurines sat on a shelf beside some books. A papyrus mat carpeted the floor. The light came from an electric bulb in a lampshade that looked like a giant candle. A laptop sat on an office desk at one end. A screensaver displayed photos of a happy family. *Jjungo's family*, Jamwa thought.

Ondego hauled himself in through the window. Jamwa followed. Ondego lifted the carpet to reveal a trapdoor, and they descended into a dark tunnel. As they groped about for a switch, the trapdoor slammed shut, plunging them into pitch blackness. Ondego clapped his hands, and fireflies appeared, enabling them to see a long, plain corridor and a monster charging at them. It looked like a hound the size of a horse.

The dog spat a fireball. It hit Ondego's chest, slamming him against the wall and setting him aflame. Ondego screamed. His fireflies went out. The hound spat another ball at Jamwa, but again all Jamwa felt was discomforting hot air. Ondego struggled to his feet and clapped a thunder that temporarily deafened Jamwa and caused the tunnel roof to collapse. Daylight poured in. Ondego threw a lightning bolt at the dog, which ducked, and dissolved into a man. He was naked, save for a necklace made out of femur bones. He spat another fireball, hitting Ondego in the chest again, and Ondego collapsed, screaming in pain.

The man plucked a bone off his necklace, and it turned into a knife. He lunged at Jamwa, who ducked, and the knife sunk into the wall. As Jjungo struggled to free the knife, Jamwa yanked a bone off the necklace. It did not turn into a knife, but it still sunk into Jjungo's back. Jjungo screamed.

Jamwa stabbed and stabbed. Jjungo staggered about. Jamwa slashed his neck open, and Jjungo fell to the ground, where he twitched and twisted as smoke rose from his skin. Then he went still.

Jamwa ran to Ondego. His body was charred.

"I'll be fine," he said, grimacing with a lipless mouth. "I just need a new body. Help me get into the sunlight."

Jamwa carried him out of the shrine and lay him on the grass, and like a snake shading off its skin, Ondego wriggled out of the charred body. He had the same face, but it was much younger, without gray beards or wrinkles.

"Thank you," he said. "Now let's get you back to the hospital."

:::

Jamwa opened his eyes. A ceiling fan stood motionless above him. He heard bleeps and turned to see a new nurse examining the display screen. He was no longer in the emergency room. He was in a private ward, still breathing through a ventilator as an IV fed fluid into his veins. The nurse smiled.

"You are awake," she said. "It's a miracle."

An hour later they allowed his family to see him. Immy and the girls came first. She had a bouquet of flowers, and the children had made him a get-well card. Their eyes shone with tears of joy. The only uncle present was Mabaga. The sight of him turned Jamwa's happiness into a bitter froth in his mouth. All he could think of was that he would not find evidence to bring the man to justice.

## ::: Monwor :::

He came to her dreams that night. He was with a much younger woman, which irked her, but he had the combined face of a pig and a monkey, which comforted her. When she woke up, something he had once said rang in her ears like the endless honk of a train.

"I'm afraid of open closets, Segolene."

He had said it the night she took him to see her parents for the first time. She could not understand why that phrase came to her, but it drilled a hole in her skull; and she flung the pillow against the wall as though that would take away the pain.

More than a year had passed since he'd left her. She hated that she was not able to move on, not able to find a new man, not able to find any peace.

Her phone rang. She jumped at it, anxious for it to distract her, but when she saw the caller ID, she hit the reject button. Her boss: the District Police Commander. He had started pestering her for sex a few days after her husband left, and it had gotten so bad that she was thinking of quitting the force. She had not slept with a man in over two years. Her husband had stopped touching her nearly a year before the divorce. The urge sometimes made her bowels dance the way steam makes a kettle's lid dance, but she could never give in to a beast like the DPC.

The phone rang again. She hit the mute button.

She staggered out of bed and drew the curtain, flooding the room with sunrise. If she wanted to forget him, she would have to move out of this home, which they had shared for ten years. Everything in it had memories of him. The curtains they bought in Owino market, the black sofas that cost her a whole month's salary, the bed covers he bought while on a UN Mission in Congo, she would have to burn it all. But she could not. Deep down inside, a hope burned that he would return.

When the phone rang a third time, it occurred to her that the DPC might be calling over work and not to spew his dirty tongue in a crude attempt to get into her pants. Still she did not answer. She did not have to go to the station for another hour.

Thirty minutes later, as she dressed, a truck stopped outside her door. She knew the sound of that engine. She took her time to answer the knocks. She wore no makeup. Her skin was pale from the bath. Only half of her hair was plaited. She did not bother to hide the mess under a cap. She opened the door. The DPC glared at her. The officer in charge of CID stood behind him.

"Don't you have money to buy a comb?" the DPC said.

"Why are you here?" she said.

"There's been a murder," the CID boss said. "Your department."

"Somebody killed his wife?" she said.

"No. A woman killed her lover."

"Why can't it wait till I get to the station?"

"When you see the body, you'll know."

When she got to the crime scene she saw why they had dumped it on her though it was not domestic violence. The men remained outside. She was alone with the corpse, which lay beside a leather sofa, naked. Something had eaten it, yet not a drop of blood had splashed. The woollen carpet bore no signs of dampness or crumbs from the feast. The body must have been eaten elsewhere, maybe several hours after death, and then dumped here.

Had this man lived alone?

A used condom peeped from beneath a coffee table. An empty bottle of red wine and two stained glasses sat on the table. A twenty-four-inch flat-screen TV blasted a Nigerian dance song. Half-dressed girls shook their bums at the camera, as though taunting the dead man. The sun came in through red cotton curtains, filling the room with a sanguine ambiance that the bloodless corpse had failed to evoke.

Segolene staggered out. In the compound two long blocks of one-bedroom rentals faced each other, a car parked in front of every door. A crowd of cops and spectators stood a safe distance away at the other end of the compound near the gate. Neighbours peered from their porches, but the two on either side of the victim were empty, the doors and windows locked. The occupants had fled as far away from the haunted rental as possible.

"This is not DV," she said, trying not to stagger as she walked to her bosses. "Something ate that man." It pleased her that her voice was steady and did not betray the turmoil in her chest.

"The last time he was seen alive was Saturday," the DPC said. "He was with a woman."

Six days? The body had shown no signs of decomposition and did not even have an odour. It could not have been six days dead.

"The wine and condom mean he was involved intimately with her when she killed him," the CID boss said. "Maybe she had a dog that ate him."

"A dog couldn't have done it," Segolene said. "No way."

"Why not?" the CID boss said.

"Those bite marks—" she said, but could not finish the sentence. "This is not my case."

"It is domestic violence," the DPC said. "A woman killed her lover."

"You are dumping it on me because you are afraid of whatever ate him," she said.

And she walked away.

The crowd parted to let her through. There was a bigger crowd outside. Her stomach rumbled. The smell of living bodies evoked images of the odourless, unrotten corpse that might have been six days dead. She could not hold it anymore. She puked. It hit the tarmac, splashing bystanders, who jumped, cursing.

They were in Senior Quarters, the most affluent suburb of town. In colonial times it had been the English section. Over the years, rental houses had been built in the vast compounds, and now there was quite a crowd of young middle-class people living behind the tall green hedges and mammoth gates.

She needed a ride back home. She could not use the only police car in sight. The driver would not take her home without approval from the DPC, and the DPC would not approve of her leaving abruptly. But the murder had attracted bodabodas. They normally did not bother to linger on this side of town. Everybody here drove their own car. She jumped on a bike. The boda man was reluctant to leave, even though it was unlikely that he would see anything.

:::

She went back home. She plaited her hair as she drank strong black tea to get rid of the taste of puke. She did not get to work until after ten o'clock. The station, an old colonial building that had seen little new paint or renovation in the fifty years since independence, showed no sign of unusual activity. She had thought the strange death would have thrown it into turmoil, but cops milled about as usual— gossiping, laughing, smoking cigarettes—and bare-chested prisoners slashed the overgrown grass in the surrounding bushes while some swept the yard clean.

Her office, a tiny room in the back, had once been a store. A few years ago, when the Ministry created the Family Protection Unit, many saw it as an anti-man establishment, something donors had forced upon the government. While liberal men in other districts treated it as a proper unit, here she suffered the consequences of not allowing the DPC into her pants. She was underfunded and understaffed. Often she was alone in the department.

The office had a large wardrobe shoved against one wall. In it, she kept files and bits of evidence. On the opposite side of the room at the other, shorter end of a rectangle was her desk, so small it might have been stolen from a primary school. Her chair had collapsed more than once while she sat on it. The door was on one long end of the rectangle. Directly opposite it was a window with wooden shutters and no curtains. A bench sat under the window. A man sat on the bench. He stood up as she wavered at the doorway, wondering what species he represented. Normally, it was a woman on that bench, telling her about an abusive husband.

"Who are you?" she said.

"He was my best friend," he said, speaking as if he had something stuck in his throat.

The eaten man?

She stomped off, went round the building to the front, and charged into the DPC's office. He lounged behind a huge chair with leather cushions. His desk alone was the size of her office.

"It is not DV!" she said. Her boots thumped the carpet as she stomped to him. She intended it to be a scream full of the anger she had bottled up following a year of sexual harassment, not a whisper. "It's not my case!"

"Do you want to be suspended for insubordination?" he said, lighting a cigarette.

"Are you men so cowardly that you dump that case on a woman?"

"No," he said, grinning. "It's because you are foolish. You think your husband will come back."

She wanted to slap him. She wanted to put a bullet in his teeth. She hated his arrogance and her powerlessness. She could not report him. She had tried, but the buffoons in Headquarters brushed aside her complaint. Off the record they had told her, "He's only courting you. If you don't like him, don't accept. If it bothers you, there are many NGOs and UN people who employ firebrand feminists."

Unable to speak anymore, she stomped out, hating herself for not having the courage to resign, just as she did not have the willpower to get over her divorce. She comforted herself that she only stayed because she loved her job. Because, even though one pig made it hell, the other female officers looked up to her as a role model, and many women slept safely at night as she dealt with their monster husbands. Quitting would be a selfish act. Things might get better. This pig might get a transfer. Maybe they would get a female DPC. Things just might get better.

By the time she reached her office, she had suppressed her anger enough to give the man there a smile; one, she hoped, that was big and friendly, even though her face was as tight as cowhide on a drum.

"She's a monwor," the man said.

"A mon—what?" Segolene said, even though she knew what he was talking about.

"The woman he picked up. She's a monwor."

Segolene collapsed onto her chair. The friendliness evaporated. She gripped the desk to hide the trembling of her hands. Veins pounded on her forehead. She hated these fairy tales that were meant to put down women. This particular one was an urban legend in many towns. It probably originated from Mombasa where Arab-influenced Swahili cultures spewed stories of jinns and creatures that came out of the sea. A man picks up a woman in the night, only for the woman to turn into a monster and eat him. Often the tales are humorous, of how, after sex, the woman elongates her arm until it is more than twenty feet long so she can turn off the lights without leaving the bed, or how the man wakes up in a graveyard, or how the man discovers that the woman's feet are like a goat's. Every town had a different name for it. Here they called it "mon ma wotho i di wor," or simply, "monwor"; the night women.

She could not understand the purpose of these stories. Were they meant to discourage men from picking up prostitutes, or was there another anti-woman agenda in the patriarchal mind of whoever cooked it up?

"If you are going to give me that piece of cow dung," she hissed, her teeth clenched, "get out."

"You saw the body," the man said.

It would explain why the men feared to handle the case. They believed they were dealing with an evil spirit that had a taste for male flesh.

"Just tell me what happened," Segolene said. "But if I hear any superstitious duck shit, I'll shoot your mouth."

She took out her gun and put it on the table. The man looked at it for nearly a minute.

"My name is Mataka," he finally said. "I have a Masters in engineering. I work in—"

"Shut up," Segolene said. "You want to say that, since you are highly educated, you don't believe in those tales, but my promise still stands. Tell me what happened. If I hear anything stupid ..." She tapped on the gun with her finger.

His throat moved up and down, as though he was struggling to swallow something and failing. The words tumbled out the way poop comes out of a constipated rectum. Ogundi, the dead man, was lonely. At thirty-eight he was unmarried and had no prospects of finding a wife.

"Why?" Segolene asked.

She had not thought that there were single men above thirty out there. Being thirty-six, she feared she would have to settle for a "second-hand man" or live the rest of her life alone, but hearing of a single thirty-eight year-old man who had no prospects of finding a wife tickled her. From the décor in his apartment, it was obvious he had money. He could have had any woman he wanted. So why was he lonely?

Mataka shrugged. "Good women are hard to come by," he said. "The young ones only wanted his money. The old ones were already married. It's a small town, you know, and soon you run out of options. So when he met Alice he got really excited.

"We were watching football. She came to our table. She said she was new in town and that she works at the Health Research Institute and that she was single. After the game he invited her to his home. She agreed. It's the last time I saw him. I didn't even get to talk to him.

"On Monday he sent a text begging me to tell our boss that he was sick. I called him back, he didn't answer. He instead texted that he was having such a good time with Alice that he didn't want interruptions. I let it be, but on Wednesday, when he still wasn't answering the phone or showing up at work, I went to his home. She let me in. He was in bed. I thought he was sleeping. She had covered him up to his neck with the blanket."

"But there was no blood," Segolene said.

"No. He just looked like he was sleeping. I couldn't wake him up. She said he had drunk too much. I accepted the explanation and left him alone. But then last night I saw her with another man. I tried to follow her, but they got into a car and drove off. So I went to his home and found him dead."

Mataka rubbed his eyes. Segolene thought he was forcing back tears. He kept his face turned away from her. Was it all a show? she wondered. Had he killed his friend and cooked up the monwor story as a cover?

:::

Bazaar Street might have been the first in town, but after a century it had turned into a ghost street, though with a postcard look. A little green mountain soared in the background, vivid against the blue sky. The derelict buildings had fresh paint after various corporations had pasted their colours in aggressive adverts.

The buildings, once meant to be retail shops, had turned into bars and restaurants as the traffic of customers dwindled. The most popular, Blue Mountain, had become a favourite hangout of the middle-class crowd. It was halfway between a proper bar and a kafunda, the part-shop/part-bar establishments that had cropped up in the eighties at the peak of a civil war when people preferred to drink closer to home. The shelf behind the counter contained bottles of beer, whiskeys, and sachets of waragi, but there were floor-to-ceiling shelves that had stocks of sugar, salt, stationery, tinned food, shoe polish, sanitary towels, nappies, and a mishmash of other products. In the evenings some patrons sat on stools at the counter, others on plastic chairs around wooden tables squeezed into tiny back rooms or on the pavement, but most preferred mats on the veranda. Being early afternoon, the place was empty of customers. Ugandan dance music boomed but failed to give life to the street.

"We met her here," Mataka said. "And last night I saw her here."

Something stirred in Segolene's heart. Was it easy to find men in this bar? Was it a favourite of unmarried men in their thirties? Could she find love here?

Two waitresses in blue shirts that revealed their big bosoms sat at a table on the veranda, giggling at something in a newspaper. One of them had dreadlocks and too much makeup on. Even from a distance, Segolene could tell she had blue eyelids. They looked up when Segolene marched to them, and the giggling stopped abruptly. Segolene thought her uniform had unsettled them. Didn't officers ever come to this place?

"Karibu, officer," one of the waitresses said, but did not stand up to welcome her. She had a tattoo of hearts and flowers on her neck. "Do you want a cold beer?" The uncertainty was clear in her voice.

"No," Segolene said. "I want to ask you questions."

The waitresses glanced at each other.

"There has never been trouble in this bar, officer," Dreadlocks said.

"Hello, ba-girls," Mataka said, only that his "girls" came out "gah-los".

The waitresses beamed at him. "We are fine, uncle,"

they chorused. "Nga, today you are walking with a uniform," Dreadlocks said. "You want to arrest us oba what?"

"I'm looking for one of your customers," Segolene said with a big smile to reassure them of her friendliness. She sat down, and Mataka took the fourth chair around the table. "If you tell me the truth, you won't be in any trouble."

"It's the woman in the maxi." Mataka asked, "You remember her?"

Segolene watched carefully, looking for any hidden messages they might exchange. Maybe he had bribed them to give credit to his story.

"Yes," Tattoo replied. To Segolene, she said, "Women hardly ever come here. When we saw you, we wondered, oba, why is this policewoman here, oba, you understand? The women who come here wear jeans or mini-skirts or something sexy, you understand? Not uniforms and surely not maxi dress, you know, so when we saw that woman we talked. It looked like a Muslim's dress—"

"No," the other said. "A maternity dress."

"It's the same thing," Tattoo said. "She did not have a burqa, but I wondered why someone would come to a bar in a Muslim's dress, if you know what I mean. But the dress was so long we couldn't see her feet."

"Naye, she wore high heels," Dreadlocks said.

"How do you know if you couldn't see her feet?" Segolene asked.

"From the sound she made as she walked," Tattoo said. "It was a kakondo. We thought it funny, why wear that dress with a kakondo? We thought she would trip and fall. It happens if you wear long dresses with kakondo. She had no sense of fashion."

"How often did she come here?"

"Twice," Dreadlocks said. "The first time was when Chelsea lost that game. Then last night we saw her again wearing the same dress. Oba, she doesn't have another one?"

Segolene still could not make up her mind whether they

were conniving with Mataka or whether indeed there was a woman in a maxi dress and high-heeled shoes. It occurred to her that a goat would make the same noise as a kakondo if it walked on pavement and that monwor were said to have hoofed feet. She shook the thought away. Had Mataka and these waitresses rehearsed the cover-up? How much had he paid them?

"Who was she with last night?" she asked.

"Mugisha?" Tattoo said. "He is a—" She stopped talking abruptly and slowly turned to Mataka. "Last week didn't she go with—"

"Yes," Mataka said. "He's dead."

They gasped. "Did she kill him?" they chorused.

Mataka nodded.

"Oh, God," Tattoo said. "We heard about a murder this morning. A man was killed, and dogs ate his body. Was it your friend?"

Mataka again nodded, and he wiped his eyes.

"Where can I find this Mugisha?" Segolene asked. "Do you have his number?"

They shook their heads in unison. "No," Tattoo said. "Naye, he comes with two friends to watch football. Isn't today Friday? They'll come at night to watch previews of the Saturday games."

"Is he in trouble?" Dreadlocks asked.

"That prostitute works with thieves," Tattoo said. "When men take them home they call up their gang, and they kill the man and steal all his property."

"She works at UTRO!" Dreadlocks suddenly screamed.

"What?" Segolene and Mataka asked in unison.

"You know her?" Tattoo asked. "How do you know that?"

"I saw a UTRO sticker on her phone. Only people who work there would put such a sticker on a phone. I mean, it's not a cool sticker like for Bell lager or Movit or MNet. It's a UTRO sticker. Either she works there, or she has some connections to it!"

Segolene's heartbeat quickened. UTRO, Uganda Trypanosomiasis Research Organization, was the old name for the Health Research Institute. In the early nineties the name had changed to Livestock Health Research Institute, and then more recently it became Health Research Institute since it no longer focused on only animal sicknesses but also on every disease that affected human beings. Yet, being a small town, the old name had stuck."That's where she said she works," Mataka said, his voice barely a whisper.

Segolene still could not decide if the waitresses were in league with Mataka. Had she just gotten a breakthrough on the case or were they feeding her false clues?

:::

They sped to the Institute in Mataka's car. It was about five miles outside of town. On the way she interrogated him to understand the nature of his relationship with the dead man. She wanted a motive. Money? Love? Jealousy? She had nothing. The two men had worked together in the Ministry of Works for over fifteen years and had grown close in that time. She would have to question their mutual friends and their workmates if she was to find a motive.

At the gates of the Institute, soldiers stopped them.

When Segolene had visited it a few weeks back, it had the feel of a hospital with a broken fence, unarmed guards at the gates, and children playing in the compound as staff milled about on their daily activities. Now, apart from the soldiers fondling AK-47s, nobody was in sight. Tall barbed wire enclosed the complex. A tent and an armoured car stood just beside the gates. Usually, since she was in uniform, she would not have had to be searched, but a soldier kept his gun trained on them while three others meticulously searched through the car. They had to walk through metal scanners and then suffered a body search and an interrogation before being let through.

"Is this now a war zone or what?" Segolene said as they parked the car.

"Maybe they fear terrorists," Mataka said.

There were three cars in the parking lot in front of the main building, a three-storied structure that resembled a city shopping mall. They passed through another set of security checks, then got into a large reception area with tiled floors and a glass counter. The receptionist wore a pink blouse with the HRI logo on the breast. She had no makeup. Her eyes were red. Segolene wondered if it was from some kind of infection. She took a step back from the counter, afraid to catch disease.

"Good afternoon, officer," the receptionist said with a strained smile. Her lips trembled, which made Segolene think she was trying too hard to keep the smile pleasant.

"We are looking for one of your staff," Segolene said. "Alice. We don't know her surname. She's in ..." Segolene trailed off, for the fake smile vanished and the receptionist's mouth hung agape. Her lips stopped trembling. Her face froze in an expression that Segolene could not place. Shock? Horror? Fear? "Are you okay?"

Tears sprang out. Now Segolene knew why her eyes were red.

"Go to the Human Resource Manager," she said, her voice strangled. She kept swallowing, as though there was a fire in her throat that she was trying to put out with saliva.

"You seem to know Alice," Segolene said, stepping closer to the desk. "Is she your friend? Do you know what she did?"

"Please," the receptionist cried. "The office ..." She pointed to a corridor and then fled into a door behind the counter, vanishing before Segolene could say another word.

Segolene glanced at the soldiers manning the glass doors. They fixed her with impassive glares, their hands on their guns. Slowly, she walked into the corridor. Her knees trembled. Her boots echoed louder than Mataka's trainers, which almost made no noise. There were many doors, all closed. Only one, labeled "Human Resource Manager," stood ajar, as if waiting for them.

A thin man with grey hair sat behind a large desk with a surface like a mirror, leafing through a file folder. A computer monitor sat on one corner of the desk. A screensaver played. It looked like a video artist's impression of viruses in a drop of blood.

"Come in, officer," Manager said. "Sit." He pointed at a two-seater sofa.

They sat right in the path of an air-con's fan. It hummed noisily and blew a gust of wind that made it difficult for Segolene to breathe.

"Turn it off if you want, officer."

The Manager pointed at a remote on the arms of the sofa. Segolene fumbled with the controls until she figured out how to turn off the air-con.

"How can I help you?" Manager said.

"You were expecting us," Segolene said.

"Yes," Manager said. "The guards at the gate told us."

"We are looking for Alice," Segolene said. "We don't know her surname, but she works here."

"Hmmm," Manager said. "What's this about?"

"Murder," Segolene said.

"Oh. That's terrible. We heard of a murder in town this morning and that dogs ate the body. So terrible. How is this Alice involved?"

"That's what we want to know."

The Manager shrugged. "We have three women called Alice. I can show you their photos. If none is the woman you want, we have a large staff here, over two hundred people. In fact, exactly two hundred fifty-six. Scientists, administrative staff, support staff, all that. The good thing is we have a computerized filing system, and we have photos of everyone."

He turned the monitor to face Segolene, then tapped the keyboard. The screensaver vanished to reveal a program. The face of an old man with spectacles and a big white beard sat at one corner of the screen. Segolene moved closer and saw essential bio-data beside the photo. Name, date of birth, address, position at the institute, next of kin, and coded data, too.

"You can look through all the photos," Manager said. "Just tap this arrow key to scroll to the next." He pushed the wireless keyboard to her.

Segolene bit her lips. This had turned out easier than she had imagined, so easy that she suspected a trap. First was the presence of soldiers, then the strange behaviour of the receptionist, and now this? She at once knew that if they scrolled through the staff list, they would not find Alice. Maybe the Institute had deleted her data. But why? Why were they hiding a murderer?

Still Segolene and Mataka looked through all the faces. They skipped the males, and Mataka studied each female long enough to be certain it wasn't the woman in the maxi dress. As Segolene had suspected, they did not find Alice.

"Maybe she no longer works here," Manager volunteered. "You see, this program only shows names of active staff." He clicked on icons as he talked and opened up another program. "We have a database of all our staff right from the time this institute opened. Many don't have photos, but if the woman you want is in her mid-thirties or younger, we have her photo, for she could only have enrolled recently. So please, look."

They looked. And still did not find her.

When Manager gave her a grin, she knew for certain that he had set it all up, that she would get nothing from him, but that receptionist ...

"Well," she said, standing up. "Thanks for your help. It seems we had wrong information."

At the reception they found an older woman with thick glasses. She wore a gomesi, a traditional dress hardly ever seen in offices, especially not in offices with tiled floors and glass walls. They were ceremonial costumes, mostly reserved for special functions like weddings. If it was old and worn, village women wore it daily. But not a woman in an office like this.

"Where is the other girl?" Segolene asked.

"She left," Gomesi said. "Her shift ended."

"So, it's your shift?" Segolene said. "But you are not in uniform."

"We are expecting special visitors, and they asked me to dress up."

"Where can I find her?"

The woman shrugged. "Come back on Monday. I can't give you her number unless the people upstairs okay it." She pointed at the ceiling. "But if you give me your number, I'll ask her to call you."

Segolene wrote her number on a yellow sticker, knowing she would never get a call. Something strange was going on here, a cover-up of some sort. Maybe they had already dismissed the receptionist or taken her far away where Segolene would never get at her. But why?

:::

Segolene did not notice the envelope until they had driven out of the Institute complex. It lay on the floor at her feet. They had not rolled the windows all the way up to let fresh air in. Someone had taken advantage of this and slipped in the envelope. She tore it open to find a sheaf of photocopied papers, most of it typed, some of it questionnaires with boxes checked, other sheets had handwritten notes. The top sheet said it was a lab report from a cancer research project. She guessed it came from the crying receptionist. Was it a gift with answers?

Segolene read the papers twice before they made sense. She could not figure out the technical terminology, but there were phrases here and there in common English from which she gleaned the essence of the report. A Dr. Masaba had designed an immunotherapy treatment for cancer and was testing it on volunteers. The volunteer in the report was only identified with a number, but her essential biodata was indicated. She was a clinical officer in the institute, twenty-six, diagnosed with breast cancer. Was it Alice, the woman they were looking for?

The treatment involved using a genetically engineered micro-organism called "Mukwasi" to identify and kill cancer cells while producing molecules to induce the immune system to destroy the tumour. It worked as expected. The volunteer was cured within two days. However, Dr. Masaba failed to remove Mukwasi from her body. Instead, it mutated into a parasite, and the volunteer developed a craving for meat. Every day, worms were extracted from her stomach, though the doctor could not trace the source of infection, nor were the types of worms mentioned.

Did the volunteer eat raw meat? Segolene wondered. Is that why she got worms?

The image of a partially eaten body floated up like something in a nightmare. Had the volunteer turned into a cannibal? She shook the thought away. It couldn't be. No human teeth could have made the bite marks she had seen on the corpse. Whatever ate Ogundi, its teeth had cut clean through raw flesh the way human teeth cut through a juicy banana.

The last page had a single handwritten word at the bottom. "Escaped." Segolene stared at it for a long time. Did it mean the volunteer had escaped? Did that explain the presence of soldiers? Were there more volunteers infected with a mutant parasite and a craving for meat? Were the soldiers to ensure they did not escape?

As she shoved the papers back into the envelope, she discovered something else inside, a passport photo with a name handwritten on the back: "Alice."

Segolene studied the photo for over three minutes: the plump cheeks, the short nose, the large eyes that appeared to be laughing. This young woman with breast cancer had volunteered, hoping for a cure. Instead, something went wrong, and she had turned into—a what? A cannibal? A monster from urban legends? An evil spirit? A monwor who stalked the streets in the night looking for men to eat?

The report was not a gift with answers. It was a question bank.

The sun was going down, draping a golden hue over the old buildings on Bazaar Street, when they returned to the bar. Music boomed, but no one danced. A man stalked a barbecue stove, preparing pork and chicken to grill, while another kneaded dough to make rolex, the most popular fast food in Uganda. A couple had settled on the veranda. They seemed bored. The tattooed waitress stood by a pillar, playing with her fingernails. She did not look up until Segolene was only a pace in front of her.

"They are here!" she said in a whisper. "We haven't told them anything!"

Segolene followed her through the bar-cum-shop into an inner room, which would have been a large bedroom but was now a football room. A twenty-four-inch TV was stuck in a cage suspended on a wall. Posters of various European football teams and African soccer superstars decorated the walls. There were four tables, but only one was occupied. Two men feasted on pork ribs and Bell lagers, their eyes glued to the TV. Someone missed a goal. They cursed as if the game was live. They did not notice Segolene until she stood right in front of them, blocking the TV.

"Hey," one said. He wore spectacles. "Please, we are watching something."

"Come sit, watch with us," the other said, leering. "I like women in uniform."

Segolene, for a moment, wondered if this man was single and searching. He looked to be in his mid-thirties with a neatly cut beard. He wore a silk shirt that revealed his nipples. He was so fat he seemed to have no neck.

"I'm looking for Mugisha," she said.

"Why?" the leering man said. "I'm as good in bed."

Segolene pulled out her gun and clicked off the safety. She put the barrel on the man's forehead. The leer vanished.

He pressed himself against the wall, trying to get away from the gun. He pressed himself so hard that Segolene thought he would sink in and vanish.

"I don't like men who joke with me," she said.

He wanted to say something, maybe to apologise, but an incomprehensible sound escaped from his throat and a line of fear showed on the corners of his mouth.

She eased the gun off his skin. The man remained pressed against the wall. She turned to the spectacled man.

"Where's Mugisha?"

"At home," he said. His voice had a slight tremble. "He's a good man."

"He'll be dead if I don't find him right away," Segolene said. "Where does he live?"

:::

The spectacled man took them to Agururu. Unlike Ogundi, who had lived in a rental, Mugisha lived in a run-down bungalow with a low wall fence. They could see the front porch through the bars on the gate. There was a padlock on the gate.

"Strange," the spectacled man said. "This gate is never locked."

He had told them that Mugisha had a family. His wife and kids had gone visiting an aunt for a few days, leaving him all alone in the bungalow. He had succumbed to temptation and picked up Alice.

"Maybe that's why he closed the gate," the spectacled man continued. "He doesn't want his wife to surprise him."

"Or maybe it's Alice, who doesn't want her feast disturbed!" Mataka said.

They called Mugisha's phone. It rang, but no one answered. They honked and used a stone to knock on the gate. Still, no response. Just when she had decided to climb over the wall and storm the house, the lights came on, warm and orange in the cold blue of gathering darkness.

The front door opened, and a woman walked out. She was a little shorter than Segolene had imagined. She wore a bathrobe and a skirt that flowed to the ground, hiding her feet. She ambled to the gate with the gait of a model on the catwalk. Like the waiters, Segolene believed she wore high-heeled shoes because she made a *tap-tap-tap* noise as she pranced to them.

"Hello, Alice," Segolene said.

Alice frowned. Then she glanced at the spectacled man, and her face relaxed. "Hello," she said to him, ignoring Segolene. "Mugisha is asleep. Come back tomorrow."

Segolene pulled out her pistol and cocked it. "Open the gate," she said.

Alice turned and ran. She was so fast she seemed to flash herself to the porch about ten meters away, but she was not faster than the bullet. It caught her in the back just as she was opening the door, and it threw her into the house.

Segolene climbed over the wall, aware that she was not as fit and nimble as she used to be. She jumped into the compound and ran to the door, holding the gun ready. She hesitated to enter, not knowing what lay beyond. The curtain swayed in the breeze. She could see a portion of the room, but not Alice. A trail of blood on the floor confirmed that she had hit the mark, and Alice, too wounded to walk, had dragged herself away.

Segolene stepped in. Now she could see Alice on the floor, leaning against a wall, breathing slowly, in pain, her eyes full of unshed tears. Her bathrobe was open. She wore nothing underneath. Her skin was the colour of grilled plantains. Around her navel the skin changed from human to—at first Segolene thought it was a cloth made from cow hide, but it was—animal skin, black, with grey fur.

Her feet were hoofed. It explained the *tap-tap-tap* noise she had made as she walked to the gate, the noise like high-heeled shoes. Hooves. Goat legs.

She bared her teeth at Segolene, and now Segolene saw how she bit off chunks of raw flesh as easily as she would bite off a piece of banana. They looked like a serrated blade. But as Alice fought off pain, her teeth became normal. Then, when she was trying to scare off Segolene, she went into attack mode and extra teeth slid out of her gum, giving her a serrated blade on each jaw.

Segolene took a step back. Her palms slick with sweat. Her finger hovered on the pistol's trigger. She looked into Alice's eyes for several seconds, only now noticing they were reptilian. The thing—Alice—hissed at her, its teeth bared, but that would be its last hiss. It stopped breathing. Its head fell on its shoulder. The lights went out of the eyes, leaving them grey and opaque. The extra teeth slid back into the gum, leaving only human teeth and an expression of pain.

Almost immediately, something started to move inside its stomach. Segolene's finger hovered on the trigger. The movement became frantic like something trapped inside was trying to get out. It pushed hard against the skin until it ripped flesh apart and pushed out its face. At first, Segolene thought it was a one-eyed caterpillar.

Was this Mukwasi?

It crawled out of Alice's stomach—a worm, a millipede, a white thing smeared in blood and goo with four antennae above the single eye that sat in the middle of its face. A compound eye like a grasshopper's. It slid out of the corpse and onto the floor. It had to be the parasite, the thing that had gone wrong with the treatment, the micro-organism that had mutated into this two-foot monster and had caused Alice to mutate as well, transforming her lower parts into a goat—goat legs, goat skin—and giving her serrated teeth.

The worm slid across the floor. Segolene thought it was looking for a new host. A good thing it was not as fast as Alice had been. Segolene fired. Its head exploded. Its body twitched and twisted as green goo filled the room with a suffocating odour. Then it lay still, and its white body turned a pale green.

She found Mugisha in bed, covered to the chin. He

looked asleep, but when she pulled the blanket away, she saw he was dead. Eaten. A thick fluid like saliva covered the wounds, which would explain why the corpse never rotted. Not a drop of blood was in sight, which made Segolene think that the creature had drained away all his blood.

# ::: The Last Storyteller :::

She woke up before the sun and flew down to the lake. They still called it a lake even though it no longer had water and a city sprawled in the basin. Most houses were shaped like fish with mouths gaping at the sky, eyes glowing, while those that belonged to the leaders looked like boats. Aya perched the bruka on a rock that fishermen on canoes had once used as a natural pier, but which now sat on top of a cliff. She looked down at the waking city. Particles of ice on the rock and on sculptures of dead trees around her caught the light from the fish eyes, giving it a pinkish hue. The heater threw a red glow onto her face, and it left her yearning for fresh air, as though she were stuck in a hole underground. The noise of early traffic wafted to her like music from the shakes of a thousand gourds. Bruka wings flapped in the city lights, sailing past the open fish mouths like prey fleeing predators.

She could not get his face out of her mind.

She could not remember him.

The sky brightened, and the city lights started to go out. Aya glanced at the thermometer and saw that the air outside had warmed up considerably. The ice had started to drip. She stepped out of the bruka, pulling a thermal blanket tight around her, and greedily sucked in the fresh air. She let the blanket slip off her shoulders, and the chill bit into her skin. She walked around, stumping her boots into the wet stone, hugging herself, rubbing her palms against her arms, and yet she could not get rid of his face.

The sun came up. For about an hour it would be nice and warm and friendly. She flipped on her hat's visor to protect her eyes, and the city transformed into a beautiful landscape, from nondescript steel structures, gray and gloomy in the mist, to a multitude of bright and happy colors as though an artbot had been playing with paint. The fish eyes now looked like gems—some were pearls, others diamonds, some marbles—and sunrays bounced off them like lights in a nightclub of dead civilizations. The last of the ice melted away. She could still see her breath, bluish against the warm sky, and she wished she could magically read her past in it. Then she would probably know who exactly he was.

She could not go back home. He was there. He said he was her husband.

Aya walked up a stone path under the sculpture of dead trees, and for a moment she wondered what it had felt like to sit under a real tree. Ancient poets described the music leaves made as a breeze rustled them and the song of birds perched on the branches and that it was considered good luck if a bird dropped shit on you. For more than a year she had wondered what it would feel like to fly her bruka alongside a bird. If the bird would know her ornithopter was a machine or if it would mistaken it for another bird. There were tales of eagles ripping drones out of the sky, but scientists and historians were not sure if the eagles thought the drones were rivals or if they foresaw their death and tried to fight back.

The first bruka took to the air nearly a decade after the last bird had gone down, so there was no way of knowing how the two would have related to each other. She had become obsessed with this relationship, and she ended up telling a story about it. She thought the protagonist was entirely from her imagination until last night, hardly ten hours after she released the veepic, when he showed up at her doorstep with an electronic flower in one hand.

It emitted a perfume that she vaguely remembered, a scent her mother had loved and hummed a tune that her nanny had sung to her when she was still in kindergarten. Her nanny claimed to have seen real bees hovering on real flowers. She claimed that they made this kind of sound as they sucked out nectar. She insisted hers was the right tune and the one they played at the museum was fake, probably from a robobee. Aya had not heard it in nearly thirty years. It soothed her, so she did not scream at seeing her protagonist in flesh and blood, nor did she slam the door in his face. She had stood there like a stone sculpture, wondering if she were having a nightmare or if someone had already seen her veepic and printed out a copy of the protagonist as some kind of joke. It had to be someone who knew her intimately, who knew how she would react to that scent and tune.

He had cut his finger and bled to prove that he was not a print. She had tried to drag up memories from the smell of his blood, and she caught glimpses of an injured man lying on the floor, a knife in his chest ... but that looked like her father.

Aya turned a dial on her helmet. The visor displayed a living mural of what this area had looked like back then with water in the lake, shacks struggling for space underneath trees, bare-chested men dragging big canoes into the water, stalls with stacks of fish, women in colorful dresses cleaning the fish. She walked up a sandy footpath to a large anthill, starkly red against the green vegetation, sat on it, and watched a half-submerged boat a few paces away choking in hyacinth, bobbing in the waves, six white birds standing on it, their reflections wavy on the water. Her veepic had come to her as she looked at this boat, at the birds dipping their heads into the water in an endless loop. She had wondered what was in the water, and she had seen a corpse. Him. And the veepic had fallen into her just like that.

Now she again looked at the white birds on the boat, watched their heads dipping into the greenish water, hoping it would trigger something, a long lost memory, an image, anything, something that would tell her that she indeed was married to the man she had imagined. Surely, the mural had answers since it gave her the story.

She stared until her eyes hurt. Nothing. Not even a reliving of the trippy exhilaration she experienced when the story came to her. Nothing. Just another image of a dead civilization.

She closed her eyes tight, willing the pain to go away.

Dead? Had it even existed? Had birds really filled the skies? Had trees and plants really grown all over the planet with all kinds of animals feeding off them? Had there really been a lake with boats and fish? What if the past was a lie? What if it had always been a gray and dreary world of stone and steel with some mega sensory implant giving the universe an illusion of color and a diversity of species?

She had experienced a historical veepic once that argued that the planet existed as it was because of *life*. That an asteroid with life, which was dying because the asteroid was too small to support it, fell on a bare planet and then life found a chance to *live*, and so it engineered the formation of water, of an atmosphere, of gravity, and over billions of years it built for itself a proper home. Life.

She turned the dial on her glasses, and when she opened her eyes again, she saw the street as it actually was: no mural, no birds, no water, no beautiful lakeside. Just plain gray steel stuck on bare gray rocks.

And hunger.

She walked away from the lakeside to a large building in the distance, which gleamed in the early morning sun. It was shaped like the shacks in the motion mural, rectangular walls and roof, rectangular windows and doors, and not for the first time she wondered why her forefathers had been obsessed with geometrical houses. The other popular design, which stood next to this building, was circular with a cone-shaped roof. She walked into the circular building.

A restaurant. She turned the dial on her visor, and the bare steel benches morphed into décor from the past—the fake past. She sat on a round, three-legged stool at a round table meant for twelve people. There were two other patrons, each at a huge table that emphasized their loneliness and each with a veepic headset over their faces, as a robotic arm fed them breakfast. Aya could tell from the icon blinking in the center of the headset that the person nearest her, whose gender she could not tell, was experiencing *Birds on a Boat*. Aya stiffened, watching the zee's body language to see if zee was enjoying the veepic, excited that it had indeed topped as early statistics had suggested. "People are hungry for a human story," one comment had said, that "It was easy to get into this story because you could feel it digs into humanity in a way storybots never can." She had been skeptical about this kind of praise, but never before had she walked into a random restaurant and found someone experiencing her veepic.

Her table beeped. A menu glowed. She tapped on an icon for breakfast, and instantly a waitress strutted out of a door at the extreme end of the room with a tray of food. Even from that distance, Aya could tell she was a print. Her eyes were green, and lights from the window bounced off her chocolate-colored mercury skin. When she was near enough Aya could hear a faint whirring from inside her and a steady *thud-thud-thud* that imitated heartbeats. The waitress gave her a smile, put the food on the table, and then glided away, her heels clicking against the steel floor. The wall opened, and the waitress vanished.

At one corner of the table, the icon of a veepic headset glowed. She tapped on it, and a yellow bag parachuted from the ceiling onto the table. She took out the headset, and the bag returned into the ceiling. She wore the headset, feeling a pinch on her nape as a sensory cable touched the implant at the base of her skull. A row of veepics presented themselves. To the left were the topping stories, with *Birds on a Boat* at number four, the only human-made story in the top fifty. The row below that was a list of veepics she had loved in the past and similar veepics she had not yet experienced from storytellers whose channels she had subscribed to. At the bottom of the screen were suggested veepics. She dithered, wondering if she could get into the number one topper, which she had not yet experienced, but she could not take him off her mind, so she decided to experience *Birds on a Boat* for the first time as a non-storyteller.

The moment she tapped on its icon, the restaurant vanished, and she ...

... is sitting on a white plastic chair in a rectangular room with a dusty floor. She is pleased to find the room packed. She glances at a picture framed on the wall to see the stats. A million experiences already and steadily counting. Music with a lot of drums and guitars throbs from a radio with creaky speakers. A bored waiter dances by himself at one end while a woman with oversized boobs and masculine beards clips her fingernails from behind a counter. Behind the woman a small service window opens to the kitchen, and Aya glimpses bare-chested cooks sweating over large saucepans on charcoal stoves. The windows are large, rectangular, with burglar-proof iron bars and yellow curtains fluttering in the breeze. Paint is peeling off the walls, which were once cream colored but are now a dusty brown. Through the windows she glimpses the world outside, houses with red brick walls and rusty iron-sheet roofs, trees whose leaves whistle in the breeze, caked with dust from the dirt road.

The table is wooden, and she feels the living warmth of the rough surface, so unlike the smooth, cold steel she is used to. The waiter brings her a menu, still dancing to the music, and she chooses a katogo of goat offals cooked with matooke. She watches other people as she awaits her order and is pleased to see them smile. The waiter brings her a clay bowl of steaming bananas and goat offal. She picks up the fork and stuffs food into her mouth. It is surprisingly hot. She tastes salt in the crunchy goat innards, pepper in the mushy bananas, tomatoes and onions in the soup, and it gives her a smile.

Her heartbeat quickens as he walks in. The door has a curtain made out of beads, which rattle as he brushes in.

He glances at her, probably realizing she is his creator. For a moment she thinks he'll not follow the script and will come straight to her table. He gives her a slight nod and walks up to a woman eating millet porridge and a mango. The woman does not smile. These two, and the waiter and the woman behind the counter, are the only characters. The rest are real people experiencing the tale.

Magara. That was the name she gave him. Last night he said his name was Obaraf, given to a person born on a day that ice does not melt at sunrise. Akello. The name she gave her. Last night he said she was called Aya. *Her* name. They were married.

He smiles at his wife. She does not smile back. She pulls a photograph out of her bag and puts it on the table in front of him. The photograph is of him and another woman. He chuckles. A storybot would have made him protest dramatically, even theatrically, not a chuckle, as if she has told a joke. This, commentators said, made the story truly human. They could read guilt in that chuckle. Akello's reaction, again, is nothing like a storybot would come up with, not overly dramatic. She smiles, picks up a knife on the table as if she is going to cut the fruit, and stabs him in the chest. Just as if she is playfully poking him. His blood squirts onto her face, but that does not take away her smile. She leaves the knife in his chest, and he slips onto the floor. She picks up her spoon and continues to eat her porridge.

Her father died like that. Her mother had stabbed him after she caught him with another woman. He lay on the floor with the knife in his chest, his blood staining the steel tiles, little Aya watching from the doorway.

Was it really her father?

Last night he had shown him the scar on his chest and said a doctor had saved his life.

She could not watch anymore. She took off the headset, and at once the restaurant vanished. She was back in a steel and sterile room, eating something bland. She could no longer taste the salty, crunchy, greasy intestines, the mushy peppery bananas, the oniony soup. Her mouth was full of something spongy. She spat, and a blob of something that looked like mucus splattered on the table. The robotic arm protruding from her plate dangled in the air, holding a spoonful of goo uncertainly. Lights blinked on the plate, urging her to reconnect.

Why could she not remember him?

She hurried out of the restaurant. The sun had grown hostile. She tapped a button on her shoulder, and her pants and shirt turned into a flowing gown that swept the ground as she walked. She turned a knob on her helmet, and it became a wide-brimmed hat. She pressed another button on her shoulder, and a sensory cable snaked out of her helmet into her nape. She no longer felt the heat. There were a few more people in the street, all with flowing gowns that made them look like daytime ghosts, their heads hidden inside gadgets that made them think they were in a town of a long-dead civilization under a friendly sun with tons of birds and animals and insects living happily with humans.

Her bruka was too hot to touch even with the sensory implant warding off the sun. She used a remote control feature on her wristband to open it. She climbed in. She tapped the button on her shoulder, and the gown transformed back into pants and sleeveless shirt while the hat retreated into being just a helmet. She checked the time and saw she still had thirty minutes before the records offices would allow visitors. She watched the city below, refusing to wear a visor to see the virtual vibrancy, instead seeing it as it was—nondescript sculptures of fish and boats. Fewer brukas flew above the open mouths, racing by too fast for her to enjoy the flapping of their wings as she had when still a little child.

The minutes passed. She tried to fill her mind with things that would make her forget him at least for the moment, but she could not get his face out of her mind nor that knife scar on his chest. She thought about her mother and wondered if she still lived in the Elephant City.

Aya had never liked that city. She thought the elephantine buildings were graceless, even repulsive. The stuffed elephants in the museum did not have that many colors. They were mostly gray with white tusks. Her mother, however, had loved to sit on the top of her building, which was a calf, and watch the herd of adults around her.

Mama would definitely have answers, but Mama would want to talk about other things, things that Aya would rather stayed buried deep in her subconscious. Had she wanted her husband completely out of her mind, just as she wanted to forget her mother? It did not make sense, for she could not afford memory surgery. She could now, with her story a topper, though she would have to wait a week, until after the credits had shown up in her account. Until then, she had to continue living in the guts of a fish too small to swallow her properly.

She had not created it entirely on her own. She had used an app that made it easy to quickly create stories that could compete with bots. She did not use a cerebral implant. She refused to have that. She did not want to become only half-human. She did not mind the sensory implant. It only messed with her senses like a drug, but a cerebral implant controlled how a person thought and often led to madness and sudden death. Some storytellers preferred it to compete against bots, and though they achieved success, audiences quickly reject the stories as being more bot than human, regurgitating the same old crap that bots had been recycling for nearly a century. Yet people needed those formulaic bot tales to survive. For a human to make an equivalent would require many years of hard work, and the results were not often reliable.

Then came the app. Paromit. She had been skeptical at first. Many software programs had come before it, and none delivered; but this was a true revolution. She simply had to type in what was in her mind, and the app would render it into an image that came alive in a virtual world.

She could not have dragged him out of her memory.

There was no way. She started with a random picture of a man she had found in the datanets and then kept instructing Paromit to add features to his face and remove others. She kept modifying it until the face of the protagonist came about as she saw it in her mind.

Had she really not dragged him out of her memory? Was he purely her imagination?

Mama would have answers.

No. Not Mama. She was not even sure if Mama was still alive, just because she did not get a notification from the Department of Birth and Death Registration did not mean Mama was still alive. The bots might have sent the message, and she deleted it unread. She could not think of Mama, she had to hope there were records somewhere that would give her answers.

She put on her headset and now she ...

... is in the Population Records Office at the Department of BDR. She wants to check for her mother to see if she is still alive, that her answers might be more satisfying than a collection of images that might not mean anything, but she can't talk to Mama. Not just yet. There is a crowd already waiting to access records, nearly a dozen people lining up to use the six data booths.

If the credits had already been reflected in her account, she would not have had to wait. She would have paid to jump the queue. Now she must wait her turn in the line. She has the option of wandering into other interesting worlds, but she thinks she deserves the torture of watching people standing in a queue in a room that's steel gray with no walls and no floor and no ceiling, with the only furniture being six blue booths.

Everybody else has a secondary headset on, and she notices with satisfaction that several of them are experiencing *Birds on a Boat*. She wonders what scenes they started at. She would have to go check the stats to see which parts people frequented the most, maybe before the stabbing when Magara and Akello are all over themselves in love. Maybe after the stabbing when Akello is in jail and in love with her cellmate and Magara is a half-human/half-robot zombie-like creature that can barely remember the love he enjoyed before his death.

The story meanders, much like real life, and if anyone started at any scene, it would not be too hard to follow, unlike some storybot stories that tried too hard to be clever or that were incomprehensible to humans, though set in beautiful and addictive psychedelic worlds.

Her turn to use a booth comes sooner than she expected, and she is thankful for it. Her fingers tremble as they hover on the keypad. What should she search for, her own records, or his? Finally, she thinks it is safer to start with her. She searches for her marriage records.

Nothing.

She searches for any memory surgeries that she might have had.

Nothing.

She sighs in relief.

She punches in his name, searches, but gets a single line on the screen. This person has never existed.

She walks out of the booth. Her knees are weak. She walks away from the queue, but the room has no visible wall or ceiling or floor, just a blank grayness, and she has gone nearly a kilometer from the booths before she remembers where she actually is. She takes off the headset and she ...

... plunged back into her bruka. The sun had grown even more hostile, and the horizon had become nothing but a white, featureless strip, the sky a sick, yellowish color, like pus.

He must be a print. Nothing else could explain him. A real-life print that bled real blood and had the scent of a real person. Maybe the machine had become so efficient that it could now print a real-life person. Maybe it had been like this all along from the beginning of time, printing out birds and animals and insects to live alongside humans until something went wrong and it could not make the prints anymore and now it had repaired the fault and was printing out real humans to replace humans.

He must be a nightmare.

Mama might know.

No. Not Mama.

Maybe Mama printed him out to force her to talk. He had, after all, told her something similar, that, when she made him the protagonist of *Birds on a Board*, she subconsciously wanted him to reconcile with her. So he had come straight to talk to her. *I never stopped loving you.* His voice sounded like a rusty engine struggling to come to life, the kind of voice that alcohol had ruined. *Even when I had your knife in my chest, I never stopped loving you, and you put the knife in my chest because you could not stop loving me.*

No!

She had gotten the idea one evening as she sat on the cliff, watching the fish city below, admiring the brukas flying over the boats. She had walked to the anthill and seen the half-submerged canoe, the birds, and the imaginary corpse under the boat. The story had fallen into her in one piece: how the man died, why he ended up under a submerged board, and that the birds were dipping their heads into the water to eat him. She had meant it as a metaphor of her own life. She imagined that she would die and would be rotten before the neighbors discovered her. Her house would know she was dead, of course. It would notify the Department of Births and Deaths and then chuck her into the recycle system. Her neighbors would only know of her death when a new tenant came in, probably months after she was long gone.

If she had lived in the past, however fake the past seemed, she would have had pets—a dog, a cat, maybe a bird in a cage—and upon her death, even if the neighbors did not know, her pets would have eaten her. If they did not, she would have ended up in a grave to feed maggots. It would be better to die in that imaginary past. It would have been better for something other than metal to eat her.

Somehow he was right. She made the film to send *him* a message.

Not him, the ghost that had shown up at her doorstep, but someone else, someone who would interpret her veepic and fall in love with her and grow old with her and probably have children with her, natural children that would grow in her womb the old-fashioned way.

Her nanny had once told her a folk story, which did not require any headsets to be enjoyed, just words falling out of her tongue, about a boy who had wished to have a friend. He sat under a tree that he did not know was a home for the ancestors. A spirit heard his wish and materialized into another boy. He was overjoyed to finally have a friend, but then it was not a good spirit and the story had a horrible ending.

If he was not a print, then he was a nightmare. He was her wish coming true.

Mama would have answers.

*No!*

Maybe *it* printed him as a gift to her.

It. Life. The machine. It needs people like her, for stories fuel its survival. It knows of her rare ability to imagine. It knows she will make better veepics if she were happier. Her house must have known how lonely she was, that she spends days not talking to anyone, refusing to commit to a relationship with anyone, so it prints him to ease her loneliness, for it knows individual parts need to bond with other individual parts to be happy. It knows that if It prints something straight out of her imagination, she would commit to a relationship with *It*.

If she went back to the records office and this time searched for him under prints, would she know the truth?

Probably.

Probably not.

Probably he was just her imagination. Her nightmare.

Mama would have answers.

*No! No! No!*

She ignited the bruka and pedaled hard as it leapt into the air, its wings flapping against its body. She flew away from Fish City, away from the sun, into the harsh whiteness of the horizon. She did not have to go back to the squalor of Fish City. She had nothing she needed there. He was still in her house, squeezed inside the guts like a worm, waiting for her, but she would not go back to him.

Everything she needed was in her bruka. With the success of *Birds on a Boat*, she could find a new house on loan. Maybe she would go to Flower City, where they ate real food that grew in special gardens protected from the sun, where they walked around without special gowns and visors because they lived in a dome that kept them safe from the environment. Surely, she could now afford it. Surely, there were enough empty apartments for her to easily get one on credit.

She would not go back home. Not to the ghost that waited for her.

# ::: The Flying Man of Stone :::

## :: Chapter 1 ::

He could not tell the colour of the trees. Rocks jutted out of the ground like pillars in the ruins of a prehistoric city, but he could not tell them from the flowers that grew wanton in the valley. Tears crawled down his face like maggots. His chest burned as though a fire bomb had been dropped on it. He could not tell if it were wind whistling past his ears or bullets. He could not hear his own footfalls nor the sound of dead twigs breaking under his soles. The thunder of gunfire deafened him. He struggled to keep up with his father, Baba Chuma, who was nothing more than a shadow fleeing through the vague shapes that he thought were trees and rocks and flowers. They could have hidden in one of the many caves on the slope, but father believed they would be safer on the plateau if the gunmen would not be bothered climbing a hundred feet to search for them.

The slope became a rock about twenty feet high. From a distance it looked like an armchair set atop a hill. Kera had climbed it a thousand times before, but now his hands were slick with sweat and he could not find footholds. His father had to help him up. Grass and thorny trees grew out of bare stone. About fifty meters ahead at the opposite edge, a grey cliff soared into the sky, forming the back of the chair. Two stone protrusions jutted out of the cliff from each end, hanging above the short trees, giving the illusion of the arms of the chair. They called this plateau Kom pa'Yamo, the seat of spirits.

Kera leaned against a boulder, winded. He squinted down the slope to check if the rest of his family—his mother, little sister Acii, little brother Okee, and elder brother Karama—were coming up the slope, too. The tears still made his vision blurry, but he could make out shapes of people running between the trees, ducking into caves to hide. He prayed that some of those shapes were that of his family, though he had seen a grenade ripping his mother apart, little Acii lying still on a pavement in a pool of blood, Okee beside her, still holding her hand tight. He prayed that he had not seen it right and that they had also escaped the massacre. The prayers brought more tears to his eyes.

He tried to look across the valley to the ledge on which their town stood. He could only see black smoke spewing from burning houses, rolling over the trees and flowers and the beautiful rocks. He closed his eyes and saw the valley as it had been just the day before, as it had always been since the beginning of time as far as he knew. A place he had visited every single day for the last three years since the war forced him out of school. An enchanting place full of boulders, some five hundred feet tall and covered with vegetation, most ranged from the size of a bull to that of a house. Many resembled household goods and animals. One gave the impression of a granary, another looked like a sleeping goat with a gourd beside it, another looked like a pot. There were hundreds of sculptures. To some people, it was a wonder of nature, especially after a group of archaeologists had failed to find evidence of a long-dead civilisation or refused to believe that a civilisation in Sub-Saharan Africa could have had the technology and aesthetics to sculpt giant stones. The locals believed it was the artwork of spirits. Nobody lived in the valley, partly because it flooded for six months during the rainy seasons. Mostly because they believed spirits lived there. So they called it Gang Yamo. Shamans had shrines in some of the caverns, and people came from distant districts to worship their ancestors.

When Kera opened his eyes, the tears had cleared. He had recovered some of his vision, but he could still see the nightmare that had befallen his town. Two tanks were rolling down the ledge into the valley in pursuit of civilians. One turned its barrel toward him and fired.

Kera saw the missile coming. He fell flat, and an earthquake shook Kom pa'Yamo. He kept his head pressed into the ground, buried under his hands as pebbles and dust showered him. The world went totally silent. He lifted his head. He could see the grass. He could feel the stones on his skin, the dust in his nose, but he could hear nothing. The two tanks were still on the ledge below the town, their barrels exploded in whiffs of smoke every few moments, but the world was silent.

"Baba!" Panic gripped him. He could not see his father. He scrambled to his feet and ran about, searching the tall grasses behind boulders, frantic. For a brief moment he feared the shell had obliterated father just as that grenade had ripped Mama to bits. When Baba Chuma stepped out from behind a boulder, Kera lost his vision again as tears clouded his eyes. "Baba," he cried.

His father said something, but Kera could still not hear.

Baba took him by the arms and dragged him through the tall grass to a cleft in the cliff that was wide enough for them to hide in. They could cover its entrance with a shrub, which would hopefully conceal them in the event the soldiers came up onto the plateau.

As they neared the cliff, they saw the mouth of a new cave. The tank round had punched a hole in the rock surface to open up a grotto. Kera had never imagined the Kom as a hollow place. He had played on it from the time he had learnt to walk. They had kicked balls against the cliff and chiselled their names on its surface, but not once had it betrayed its hollow secret.

Baba sped to it at once. Kera followed, also seeing it would offer a better hiding place than the open air cleft. They ran over rubble and slid down into the cave. Sunlight fell around its mouth, but the rest of it remained in pitch darkness. Something on the walls made him frown. It looked like charcoal drawings, but it could have been shadows dancing. He took a step back. Before he could flee, a sound erupted, like the scream of a cricket. He had regained his sense of hearing. He once again became aware of the sounds of soldiers massacring civilians, the rattling of automatic rifles, the thunder of tanks, he thought he could hear a scream.

"Get in!" His father grabbed his arm again and yanked him into the darkness.

The chill confirmed that something was not right. It was not the kind of cool he enjoyed under a tree in the middle of a scorching day. It was the kind of cold that gripped him whenever he had malaria. He jumped out of the darkness back into the sunrays, which stopped just inside the mouth of the cave. He could feel the warmth falling on his skin like something solid.

"Don't be afraid," Baba said.

"It's cold," said Kera.

"Yes. The sun has not touched its inside since the day it was created. Come. We'll be safe in here."

Kera pointed to the walls. He now got the impression that the drawings were wriggling like earthworms when cut into two, maybe in pain, and he thought they were trying to get away from the sunlight to slide into the darkness. They were strange patterns, circles that looked like triangles. He could not be sure, for the lines shifted endlessly, but it reminded him of the rock art he had seen in Nyero when his school visited pre-historic sites. Out of the shapes he started to make out animals, strange animals, stranger birds, people hunting, a woman giving birth, a child fishing. It was like watching a silent video, the characters repeating the same actions in an endless loop of agony.

"This is evil," Baba said.

They scrambled over broken stones, climbing out of the cave. Then a strange sound came from deep behind. It sounded like the hiss of a punctured tire. Kera kept scrambling out, but Baba stopped and was squinting into the darkness, trying to see the source of the sound.

"Don't stop, Baba!" Kera said.

Then he saw it, a shape blacker than the darkness, a human-like creature with a tail. It looked like one of the drawings had come off the wall.

"Baba!" Kera screamed.

Too late. In a split second the tail shot forward, wrapped itself around Baba Chuma, and yanked him out of sight. The hissing stopped all of a sudden.

Kera froze, wondering if it was all a dream.

The day had started like any other. He woke up to take goats into the valley to graze. His mother was already baking samosas to sell in her kiosk, his little brother Okee and little sister Acii sat beside her eating porridge. His older brother Karama had left to hoe the gardens. His father was at his garage, forging metals into works of art. They called him Baba Chuma, the father of metals, for he was a gifted artisan. The war was far away from their town, and there was no hint it would ever come to them. With a population of only about four thousand stuck in a sea of ancient rocks, they had nothing to offer the warlords. Then soldiers came for recruits. When no one volunteered, they shot the women and kidnapped the men. Kera had watched a grenade rip his mother apart. He had watched Okee and Acii running hand in hand until bullets sent them crashing onto the pavement. He did not know what had happened to Karama. Maybe he was dead, too. Now something that looked like a charcoal drawing had taken the only family he had left.

"Baba," he said, barely able to hear his own voice.

No response. Only a silence. Baba Chuma had not even yelled when the thing took him.

Then he heard the hiss again like a whispering of wind, like the singing of leaves, and he saw drawings moving in the darkness like smoke dancing. He fled from the cave. He stumbled over the stones on the plateau. He fell, scraping his knees, but he ignored the pain and ran fast down the slope. It was true, after all. It was not just another fairy tale, not just another superstition. The valley was a home of spirits. He had seen them. They looked like charcoal drawings and spoke like wind.

The tank cannons still pounded away from across the valley. There were still soldiers prowling about, but Kera did not stop to think about that. He would rather end up a captive of soldiers than of that charcoal thing. He sped, aware of the dangers of running fast down a slope, but he could not slow down. Evil drawings had taken his father. Evil drawings wanted to take him, too. He stepped on a loose rock, slipped, fell, and went tumbling down the slope, down, down, down, until he crashed against a tree trunk. He struggled to his feet, ignoring the pain that blazed through his body, but he could not continue running. Something grabbed him and pulled him into a cave.

He screamed. A hand clamped his mouth. He fought, struggling to get away, screaming, even as his brains registered that it was human hands—not a tail—pinning him to the ground.

"Quiet!" someone growled. "The soldiers will hear you!"

He could not stop screaming. He could not stop fighting. Shadows loomed over him. The drawings. The evil spirits. His legs kicked out. His hands broke free, and he threw a punch at a shadow. He tried to wriggle away, but a rock smashed into his head. The world turned into darkness and silence.

And dreams.

He was with his father in a place without light. Yet they could both see, the way cats see in the night. Living pictures materialised on the ragged walls, telling stories of an ancient people, of a world where magic and gods still lived with humans. The drawings rippled over the rock face like water. He got a strange feeling that he, too, was a drawing, a work of charcoal, that he, too, was made of smoke, not flesh and bones, and that he was living in an ancient world that held the secrets of the universe. It might have been a sweet dream, for this world was a paradise where he could fly, but human-like creatures with tails hissed all around him.

"Baba!" he screamed.

He woke up, strapped to the ground, supine. Red sun beams fell into the cave onto roots that had broken through the stone surface and hung suspended like the disembodied fingers of the hissing creatures. He screamed again, but not a sound came from his mouth. He was gagged. The cloth tasted of mud.

"He woke up," someone said. He knew the voice, the man everybody called Lafony, the teacher. He had taught in the primary school for forty years.

"Kera," another voice said. It belonged to Asiba, the mayor. "Are you okay?"

"Thank God," someone else said. "I feared he'd never awaken."

There were about twenty people crowded around him. He recognised them all. He listened for the sound of gunfire. Nothing. A few birds made a racket, a monkey squawked. The sun was going down. He had been unconscious for the whole day, for it had been morning when the soldiers attacked. Darkness would soon come down, and then what? Would the drawings come out of their cave?

Kera fought his bondage, but it came to him that if he wanted to flee, he would have to convince the refugees to untie him. They were not the enemy. They kept him tied up to ensure he did not give away their hiding place. He held his breath for several minutes, gaining control of his nerves, and then lifted up his hands in a gesture begging for them to untie him.

"Will you stay calm?" the teacher asked.

Kera nodded. The teacher removed the gag.

"There are spirits," Kera said, slowly, fighting to contain the panic that threatened to overwhelm him again. He wanted to say more, to tell them that the valley was indeed a home of spirits, that soldiers had knocked open the door of hell and that demons would soon be swarming the place. The only words he could manage were those three.

Someone chortled. The teacher frowned at that person, and the laughter died out. They had not seen it. Though they called the valley Gang Yamo, no one really believed that spirits lived there. Even the teacher, who openly denounced Christianity and Islam and championed indigenous African faiths, had once said that, just as God and Allah did not really live in churches and mosques, the valley was merely a symbolic place of worship.

"I saw them," Kera said. "They took Baba."

This time more than two people chortled. The teacher smiled at him.

"Why are you scared?" the teacher said. "If you saw spirits, then you saw our ancestors. You shouldn't fear them."

Kera's jaws tightened. It would be pointless to argue, to tell this man about the drawings. So he stayed quiet as the teacher untied him.

"I blame the mzungu," the teacher was saying in a low voice. "He has made us afraid of our own ancestors. Maybe this boy has seen spirits, but why should they scare him? I'll tell you why. Christianity has made us so stupid that we think our ancestors are demons. The sad thing is that this stupidity ensures the mzungu continues to rule us. You think this war is because one tribe wants to rule the other? No! It's a direct result of his greed. He created hatred between us, so instead of working together we fight each other. The chaos allows him to control the diamond mines and the gold mines and the oil fields. That's what this war is about. We are too stupid to see it. We've become so stupid that we think our ancestors were Jews and we think our true ancestors are demons."

Now free, Kera rubbed his wrists where the rope had bitten into his skin. He examined the entrance. He could not dash out. He was at the back of the cave, and there were people between him and the mouth. They would stop and tie him up again.

"I've to pee," he said, his voice hoarse with thirst.

The cave was too small for him to use any part of it. They would have to let him out. No one heard his request for the teacher was going on about wazungu and the war. Kera stood up. That got him attention.

"I'm dying," he said. "I have to go."

A man parted the leaves that they had used to hide the entryway, then peered out, checking for signs of soldiers. The sun had gone down. Smoke from the town tinted the blue of dusk with a black mist.

"Stay close," the mayor said. "Don't scream if you see a yamo."

A few people chuckled. Kera ignored them. Once out, he ran fast down the slope. They shouted at him, but only briefly. They were afraid the noise would attract soldiers. He knew they would not follow him. This time he watched his step and ran with care. Soon he was off Kom pa'Yamo and running on flat ground through waist-high undergrowth in a small forest. Though the trees did not grow thick, their shadows made it dark.

He did not stop running until he reached a small river. Being the dry season, it was down to a trickle, deep only to the knees. If he crossed it and continued northwards up the ledge on which the burning town stood, he might meet the soldiers. Yet to the south were rocky hills bare of vegetation, some a thousand feet high. They formed a wall as though to protect Gang Yamo. To the east and to the west were vast swamps that flooded the valley during the rains. The river ran westwards from one to the other, dividing the valley into two parts. Since the army barracks was somewhere in the west, the best option was to go east. He would have to stay in the valley until he reached the swamp and either steal a fisherman's canoe to row his way across or climb the ledge and hope there were no soldiers about. Such a journey would mean passing by hundreds of spirit rock shapes and scores of boulders in which hissing creatures could be hiding. That left him with only one option: to wade across the river and return to town. The soldiers might still be up there, but that was a better fate than the hissing creatures.

*Kera,* his father said.

The voice ripped through his flesh and froze his bones. He nearly fell into the water. He searched the grass, squinted at the smoke rolling lazily beside the tree trunks, enshrouding the boulders, but saw no sign of Baba Chuma.

*Kera,* the voice came again, a gentle whisper, a soft and warm cooing. It was inside his head. Yet it was so clear, as though his father had spoken aloud.

Then he heard the brush of cloth on grass, gumboots crashing twigs, and a silhouette walked out of the blue haze. Baba's hair always had streaks of gray, his hoary beard always looked like a sponge on his chin. Now white cotton covered his head, and his beard looked like feathers of a bird beaten by the rain. He had grown younger. The muscles were firmer on his biceps, and his eyes—his eyes—they shone like metal in bright sunlight.

It could not be Baba. Kera wanted to flee, but fear made his feet sink deep into the mud, rooting him to the banks of the river.

"It's me," Baba said. "Don't be afraid."

Baba had a bag, a heavy bag that strained the muscles of his hand. In the half light Kera could not tell its colour. It looked brown, but it could have as well been blue. It was made from animal skin, maybe a goat. Had he gotten the bag from the cave of hissing creatures?

"I look different," Baba said. "They touched me."

*They didn't touch you,* Kera thought. *They transformed you.* He wanted to say this aloud, but he could not find his voice. A metallic ball sat in his throat. Yet Baba heard it and gave him a slight nod.

"They transformed me, but they are not spirits. They are just people."

*People with tails? People who look like charcoal drawings?*

"Yes," Baba Chuma said. "They are still people."

Only then did it strike Kera that Baba could read his mind. His mouth became so dry that he could taste fire. He could not feel his body anymore, only his heart beating like a madman banging his head against a brick wall.

"The soldiers are gone," Baba said, as he resumed walking. "The town is safe. Come with me. I need your help in the workshop."

Baba did not wait for a response. He lugged the goatskin bag and plunged into the river. It seemed to weigh a thousand kilos, though it was no bigger than the basket his mother used to take to the market.

*What is in that bag? What makes it so heavy?*

Kera did not want to follow his father. Questions whirled in his head, fuelling his terror. What kind of people could change the appearance of a man? Why had they given him the bag? What was in the bag? What work could be so urgent that he had to go to the workshop in the night? Yet there would surely be corpses in the streets. Bodies of people they knew, of their neighbours, their friends, of his mother, of Okee and Acii.

*Come*, Baba said. *Don't be afraid.*

Kera remembered the dreams of the drawings and the teacher's talk about Christianity and their ancestors. If the hissing creatures were evil, they would have killed Baba or turned him into a terrible monster. Instead, they had only changed his hair and eyes and made him look younger. They had given him telepathic powers and a goatskin bag with mysterious contents. There was yet no sign of evil.

Blood resumed circulating in his legs. Now he could feel the mud beneath his feet, warm and ticklish. He did not want to, but he stepped into the river and followed Baba.

By the time they reached Katong, complete darkness had fallen. Flames leapt high off a vocational school, painting the town orange. Opposite it, the shell of a hotel gaped. A bedsheet stuck in the rubble fluttered like a flag. Burnt vehicles littered the road. A charred hand stuck out of the driver's window of a school van. Kera thought it might have belonged to Musta, who drove Acii to kindergarten. Only two schools—one for primary level and the other for kindergarten—had stayed open through the war. The town folk paid the teachers in kind, mostly with food. Kera's school, a boarding of secondary level, was in another district sixty kilometres away. It had closed as fighting spread. Apart from Musta, the van was empty. It had not picked up any children when the soldiers came.

They avoided Main Street, where they were sure to find Mama, Okee, and Acii. They used its backstreet, an alley with wooden doors leading to courtyards, some of which were business premises, but most of which were residences. Here the darkness hid the identity of the dead. They saw a corpse in a gate that stood ajar. Kera luckily did not know anybody who lived in that courtyard. They found another in the gutter, chocking the flow of water, and a third beside an overflowing garbage bin. The workshop stood at the end of the alley. The metallic gate was ajar. They went in. One side was a graveyard of cars that Baba hauled in to cannibalise their parts and bodies. The other side was a roofed shelter where Baba worked. Since school closed Kera had taken to helping him in the foundry.

"There are no corpses here," Baba said.

*How do you know?* Kera wanted to ask. He only swallowed and watched Baba lug the bag to the work table. All along, Kera had stayed behind Baba so he would not have to see those frightful eyes. Now Baba wore a pair of black welding goggles. Kera sighed in relief. He would not have to look into those eyes.

Kera flicked on a switch. Several bulbs came on. They drew power from a solar charged battery. Baba opened the bag. Kera froze in anticipation, but it was only full of rocks. Not ordinary rocks, though. They looked like glass with shades of green, yellow, and black, each the size of Baba's fist.

"Start the fire," Baba said, giving him one of the strange rocks. "Melt it."

*What are we going to create?* Kera wanted to ask.

He did not.

Like a puppet, Kera followed instructions. They worked all night. Kera melted the strange rocks, as well as iron and steel, and planed timber. Toward midnight what they were building started to take shape. At first, Kera thought it would be a two-wheeled cart roughly the size of a coffee table. They completed it as the first lights of dawn appeared. It was some kind of machine. A tube whose insides were lined with sheets of the strange glass rock passed through a box, which had an engine. The box and tube sat on the bed of the cart. At one end of the cart, there were levers. At the other end there were six projections that looked like arms complete with fingers.

*What does this thing do?* Kera wondered.

His eyes were dry and aching, eyelids heavy with exhaustion and muscles throbbing with a dull pain. A wind blew, stinging his nose with the smell of ash and bodies that had started to rot. He thought they should go to the street to gather up his mother, Okee, and Acii, who would by now be swathed in flies. He thought they should give them a decent burial before the worms turned them into obnoxious objects. He had not thought about them all night. Even now he pushed away the horrible images, as though they were something he had seen on TV.

Baba Chuma hooked a battery onto the machine and flicked on a switch. It gave a low hum. Kera stepped away, expecting it to transform into a monster and eat him up. Then Baba picked a hammer and pushed it into one end of the tube. The machine sucked the hammer into the box. A rattling erupted. The machine vibrated so much that Kera thought it would fall to pieces. A light flashed inside the tube. It made Kera think of a photocopier. He thought it would crush the hammer, shred it, do something to it, but it came out whole at the other end of the tube.

Kera frowned. What was the point of passing the hammer through the machine? He got an answer soon.

It turned his bones to ice. The photocopier light flashed again, and another hammer, an exact copy of the first with the same scratches on its head and the same crack on its handle popped out. Then another and another and another, replicas of the hammer fell out and piled onto the ground.

A replicating machine?

The technology he knew, like cars and computers, had intricate engines. Even wristwatches had a complex system. His father had built something straight out of a sci-fi movie. Yet its system was no more complex than that of a rope pulley. It had to be magic, Kera thought, as he eyed the glass rocks in the goatskin bag. He had melted only a few of them. The bag was still nearly full. Magic. Nothing else could explain it.

Baba pulled a lever, and the machine went silent. The hammers stopped falling out. He pushed his hand deep into the tube and took out the original hammer. A smile wavered on his mouth.

"They are ancient people," Baba said. "They have survived from a very long time ago."

For a few seconds Kera did not understand what Baba was talking about. Then it came to him. The hissing creatures. *Ancient people*, Kera thought, recalling the hieroglyphs on the cave, the rock art that was alive with timeless stories.

"They live inside the rocks because they are afraid of the sun," Baba continued. "It kills them. After the tank blew a hole into their home, they feared the sun would wipe them out. They asked for my help. They touched me and gave me their knowledge so that I can seal the hole, but they also want me to protect the valley. Come, let's push this thing to the Kom."

Words welled in Kera's throat—questions, warnings, suspicions—but not a sound escaped his lips. Baba rolled the replicator out of the workshop, not waiting for a response, not looking back to check if Kera was following.

Kera wanted to lie on the floor and fall asleep, but again his legs moved of their own volition.

He kept his eyes on the back of his father's head. That would save him from seeing the corpses in the alley, but he could not avoid the smell. It churned his stomach. He did not spit or vomit out of respect. He thought it was a good thing that there were no wild dogs in the area. They would have mauled the bodies, leaving entrails all over the place. There were no carrion crows either. The war had created hundreds of other feasting sites for the birds.

"Wait here," Baba said when they were out of town. He went back into town and returned shortly after with a small bag of cement and ropes. They continued on their way to Kom pa'Yamo.

The sun kissed the valley. A breeze licked Kera's face. Flowers blossomed, and white butterflies floated over the foliage. A wood pigeon sang. The ambience pushed the sight of the burnt town and the smell of carnage into the distant memory of bad dreams. Kera caught himself smiling. Almost at once, guilt overwhelmed him. He should not have been happy in such a morning, but as they pushed the replicator up the steep slopes to the plateau, a macabre happiness gripped him. If Baba could invent a replicator, was he then not able to bring the dead back to life? Could he not invent a machine to resurrect Mama, Okee, and Acii?

They heaved and huffed, and the replicator went slowly up and up. Whenever they stopped for a breath, they tethered it to tree trunks to prevent it from sliding back down.

"I should have built a flying machine," Baba said during a break.

*What about a machine to bring Mama back to life?* Kera thought.

"An aeroplane?"

"No. Aeroplanes pollute the world and cause climate change, but I can build a flying machine that truly imitates birds."

Kera saw his reflection in the dark glass of Baba's goggles, an image painted the colour of fire, for the sun was rising behind him.

*Maybe Baba is dead,* he thought, *and something, that hissing creature, has taken over his body.*

He had never heard Baba talk of pollution. The only English words he spoke before that morning were "Hullo," "Fine," and "Sorry." Baba never went to formal school. He learnt how to work metal as an apprentice to his grandfather, who bequeathed to him the workshop. Yet, here he was talking about aeroplanes and pollution and saying "climate change" in English. How could this be his Baba? The body might have been his, but inside it was someone else, or something else, something that knew about aeroplanes and pollution.

That hissing creature.

*Bring Mama back to life,* Kera said, but again it was only in his head.

He knew Baba had read it in his mind from the way his face twitched, but Baba did not respond. He resumed pushing the replicator up the slope. Sweat glistened on his skin. Kera pulled the machine. Every muscle ached.

There were people still hiding in the caves. Every time they passed by one, they told them that the soldiers were gone and it was safe to go back to town. Most crept out silently and started back to their ruined home with only a mild curiosity about the replicator. No one asked aloud why they were pushing it up Kom pa'Yamo until they reached the cave in which the teacher and the mayor were hiding.

"Is that a gun?" the teacher said.

"No," Baba said.

The teacher's frown deepened. "What is it then?" he said.

"Nothing," Baba said.

"What happened to your hair?" the teacher said. "Did you dye it? Why are you wearing goggles? What is wrong with your beard? Where are you taking this thing?"

"You look younger!" the mayor whispered.

"I'll explain later," Baba said.

He resumed pushing the machine. Kera thought the teacher and the others would follow, but they did not. They stood still, watching, until the trees and undergrowth hid them from view.

By the time they heaved the replicator onto the plateau, the sun had risen high and not a cloud was present to mask its heat. Baba had covered the hole in the cliff with shrubs to protect its secret, but the hissing creatures were lucky the cliff faced north. If it had faced east or west, the sun's rays would have poked deep into the cave.

Kera tried to peep into the darkness. The pictures still rippled on the walls, but he could not see the tailed people nor hear them. He could feel them, though, their chilly aura, and he suspected that Baba was communicating with them using telepathy.

Their work lasted about an hour. They replicated water, which they found in a small puddle, then stones and cement, which they used to seal the cave. Now Kera saw the other function of the machine, particularly the purpose of the six arms. They were builders. Baba manipulated them using the levers. They piled rocks and mixed cement to seal up the hole. Lastly, Baba replicated a huge pile of rocks and stacked these up to hide the cement.

## :: Chapter 2 ::

Katong town cropped up in the 1930s during the construction of the highway from the capital in the west to the mineral rich northeast, at first as a worker's camp, for it was at a midway point between the two locations. After the highway was complete, Indian traders came to make money off English colonial governors and mine owners, who had set up homes so they could have a place to spend a night on the eighteen-hour journey between the city and the northeast. As the town flourished, a quasi-apartheid system cropped up with a T-junction separating the three different peoples.

The business district had the uninhabited valley to its south and the highway to its north. Here the Indians lived in little apartments above their shops and restaurants. On the other side of the highway were the two suburbs, separated by a road that led to farms. The English lived in grand mansions in Senior Quarters, which had churches and a recreational complex with a cinema, swimming pool, and golf course. The Africans lived in Chandi, which translates to poverty, or misery, then an overcrowded slum with muddy pavements.

While a few rich Indians had mansions in Senior Quarters and a few poorer Europeans owned shops and restaurants in the business district, Africans could not live in Senior Quarters nor run any economic activity in the business area. They worked the English-owned farmlands, growing cotton and tea, and they supplied Indians with fresh vegetables and foods. They were servants and shamba boys for the foreigners.

There were two primary schools, one for the foreigners, and the other for Africans. In the two churches, Catholic and Anglican, both in Senior Quarters, the Europeans took the front rows, and the Africans occupied the back seats. Both Indians and Europeans kept to themselves, refusing to intermarry with the Africans, refusing to assimilate. After Independence they both kept British citizenships and passports.

This quasi-apartheid system survived until 1975, when the General assumed power through a military coup. He expelled all foreigners from the country. "You are milking the cow without feeding it," he said. He nationalised the mines, the oil wells, and all foreign-owned assets and gave the Indian shops to Africans. He became an instant hero. Many Africans moved out of Chandi to Senior Quarters and the business district. Those who remained had more space for themselves. The slum evolved into a low-cost suburb. "That," the teacher once told Kera's class, "is when we got our true independence."

The General ruled for twelve years—until the Americans blew up his plane as he flew to Libya. Five years of turbulence followed. One bloody coup led to another bloody coup with the country tottering close to an all-out civil war until one leader undid all that the General had accomplished. He gave the mines and oil wells back to the Europeans, and he invited the Indians to reclaim their lost property. Riots broke out, but the President had American money to bribe the opposition to his side. Three hundred civilians died before the rest got the message and stopped rioting.

The Indians and the English did not return to Katong. In the early 1990s, with a loan from the World Bank, the government built a new road to reduce access to the mineral rich region by five hundred kilometres, by-passing Katong. Now there was nothing to attract anyone to Katong. The English farms had long been abandoned. The population fell from over forty thousand to under five thousand.

The President ruled for over two decades. Then at the behest of his American masters, who wanted to prove to the world that they were doing good to the country, he organised elections. He lost to a soldier, a Colonel who had been the General's vice president. Either he made the mistake of granting the Electoral Commission total independence or they were aware of the Colonel's power, so they announced the results. Furious, the President annulled the results and ordered the arrest of the entire Commission. Again riots broke out. This time disgruntled soldiers who had been kicked out of the national feast sided with the Colonel and the rioters. Before anyone could understand what was happening, the civil war that had been threatening since the General's death finally broke out. A score of different factions cropped up to claim power and fragmented the country into territories under the rule of warlords.

The war did not come to Katong. It had nothing to attract the warlords—no wealth, no military value—it was stuck in the middle of nowhere. They ignored it—until they realised it could offer them recruits.

:::

The cemetery lay in a grove about a mile outside of town on the old highway to the city. About five hundred survivors had gathered to bid farewell to the dead. Branches of tall trees intertwined to roof the cemetery, for it was taboo to rest the dead under open skies. The coolness reminded Kera of the chill in the cave. A thick undergrowth of flowers emitted a sweet perfume, but that could not mask the odour of forty-three corpses. A hymn punctured with wails and the sound of digging wrung tears out of Kera's eyes.

The dead lay in neat rows, wrapped in bark cloth. Though they had adopted the Christian custom of scribbling the name of the deceased on a cross, they never used coffins and never sealed the graves with cement. Instead, they retained their old rituals of ringing the new home of the departed with stones and flowers. An Anglican reverend led the service. The absence of the Catholic priests was conspicuous.

Kera and his father stood over their three loved ones. Mama's face had grown blacker with death, her braids seemed longer than he remembered, and her lips appeared a little redder, as though she had applied lipstick. The bark cloth hid the rest of her body, but it was stained with black goo. Kera could only imagine the damage the grenade had done. Okee and Acii lay beside her, no longer holding hands.

*Bring them back to life*, Kera prayed silently, not to God, but to his father.

The replicator could not clone living things. He had experimented with a grasshopper. He got hundreds of insects, but all were dead. All were made of the glass rock material rather than of flesh. If he put his mother or Okee or Acii in the replicator, they would not resurrect. Instead, he would create statues.

"Never try to clone a living thing," Baba had said in a voice so soft, so unlike the alcohol-roughened voice Kera had heard all his life. "You'll only succeed in creating evil."

*Please build a machine to bring them back to life*, Kera now prayed. Baba frowned at him, but Kera persisted in his prayers. What could be so evil in bringing loved ones back to life?

"You have me," Baba said, "and Karama."

"Where is Karama?" Kera said.

"He's not dead," Baba replied.

That brought more tears of relief. He still had an elder brother. He did not ask how his father knew. He looked through the trees to the valley, which lay just beyond the old highway, wondering if Karama was hiding somewhere down there or if he had joined the small stream of refugees making their way to safer places, wherever that may have been. Had Baba had telepathic contact with Karama? Is that how he knew Karama was still alive?

*The soldiers took him*, Baba said, speaking inside Kera's head. Every time it happened, a breeze blew through Kera's skull, ice made his spine tighter, and a fire hollowed out his belly.

The revelation brought bile to Kera's mouth. If soldiers had taken Karama, he was as good as dead, for the soldiers would turn him into a monster, a rapist, a cold blooded killer, a senseless automaton who saw no value in human life and whose only purpose in life was to fight to the death for the warlords.

*He won't turn into a monster*, Baba said. *You'll rescue him.*

"What?" Kera said.

*I'll show you how.*

Kera's eyes grew several inches wider. If soldiers had taken Karama, they held him in an open-air prison with hundreds of guards. How could he, a boy not yet sixteen, rescue his brother?

Baba gave him a smile, and Kera thought an explanation was coming; but the sound of an approaching car broke the moment. A chill spread through the graveyard as a sudden hush fell upon the mourners. The digging stopped. Everybody stood still. The war had created a severe fuel shortage. Very few people could afford to drive, and most were soldiers.

"Stay calm," the teacher shouted. "It's only one car."

The teacher was inside a grave, digging, bare chested, his trousers folded to the knees, his hands and legs covered with dirt, his face smeared with mud and sweat. The slight tremble in his voice did not calm the growing panic. The doubt on his face fanned the fear. A single car could do as much damage as a convoy. It could be a pickup truck with a machine gun on its bed or a saloon with a couple of automatic rifles inside.

"Is it soldiers?" Kera asked his father.

"No," Baba said, raising his voice so those around him could overhear. "It's the wazungu from the missionary."

"How do you know?" Okello said. He was a retired policeman with pure white hair.

"From the sound of the engine," Baba said. "I know because I've repaired that car before."

"It's not soldiers!" Okello shouted to stem the growing panic. In spite of his age, his voice boomed with authority. "I know that engine! It's Father Stephen's car!"

People turned to the old man, uncertainty in their stares, and he in turn threw suspicious glances at Baba. Before a stampede could break out, the car came into view, a Landrover with a sleek blue sheen that gleamed like a pearl.

"Father Stephen!" several people shouted at the same time.

"That bastard," the teacher hissed. He climbed out of the grave and started to march toward the Land Rover, brandishing a hoe.

"Don't," Baba said, running after him. "He didn't do it."

The teacher did not stop until Baba grabbed him. A vein pounded against the teacher's temple, and Kera thought the teacher would shove Baba aside and charge at the mzungu, but the teacher did not. His fingers tightened on the handle of the hoe.

The car stopped at the roadside. Father Stephen got out and waddled toward them. He had white hair that flowed down to his shoulders and a big white beard that dangled over his chest. His skin was red with sunburn. The frock, hanging loose on his body, could not hide his obesity. His neck had vanished, and his head sat on his shoulders like a melon on a rock. He had lived in Katong for over forty years. When the General expelled Europeans and Asians in the seventies, he stayed as the church had interceded on behalf of foreigners in its service. Father Stephen was fluent in Luo. Two nuns came with him. One Italian, the other French. They had not yet learnt Luo, but they spoke good English. A hymn broke out to welcome them.

"Bastard," the teacher hissed again. But he was calm, so Baba released him.

Father Stephen exchanged greetings with many of his congregation as he waddled to the row of corpses. The short walk left him breathless.

"Oh, dear," he said. "Oh, dear. Oh, dear."

"Did you send the soldiers?" the teacher said, speaking in English.

Father Stephen's face folded. His eyes seemed to disappear beneath slabs of fat that had once been brows. His lips twitched, searching for an answer, but only a sigh came out. A few people heard the question. They frowned. The majority were out of earshot. They continued to sing and to wail.

"Hello, teacher," Father Stephen managed to say, in Luo. His voice trembled.

"Don't foul our language with your tongue," the teacher

said in English. "Answer me. Did you send soldiers to kill us?"

"What are you talking about?" Father Stephen insisted on speaking in Luo. So the exchange happened in two languages.

"Did they attack your church?" the teacher said.

"No," Father Stephen said. "No. Of course not. God protected us."

"God? Are you trying to say there is no God in the Anglican church? The soldiers bombed it. They killed the reverend's wife and his four children. There they are." The teacher pointed at a group of corpses beneath the reverend's feet. "Every building in town has bullet holes. Every family lost something. Why did the soldiers spare you? Is it because you are a mzungu? Is it because they are working for you?"

"Nonsense," Father Stephen said. "I came here to pray for the dead, and I won't let your madness stop me. This is my home as much as it is yours. Whatever madness has gripped you, I'll pray for God's mercy to touch you."

The teacher's hoe struck Father Stephen in the temple. Blood splashed onto Kera's face. The fat man crumbled to the ground with a yelp of pain. He rolled about on the ground. He would have fallen into a grave if he were a little smaller. The teacher kicked him, trying to shove him in. He brought the hoe down, intending to hack off the fat neck. Baba jumped and grabbed the teacher. Two other men joined the fray. They restrained the teacher, who fought but could not match three men. They pinned him against a tree and took away the hoe.

"You sent them!" the teacher shouted, now speaking in Luo, as he struggled against the men holding him. "You think we don't know your schemes? You want our gold and diamonds and oil! That's why you are here! You bring your stupid religion and you make us stupid and you think we won't ever know the truth? You sent them!"

The nuns helped Father Stephen to his feet. One ripped off her habit and pressed it against the wound to stop the blood. The singing stopped, people were crowding, questions flew about to add to the confusion.

"Oh, God," Father Stephen wailed.

"You dirty demon, the soldiers work for you!" the teacher was shouting.

"It's best if we left," one nun said, trying to pull Father Stephen away.

"I'm not leaving," Father Stephen said. "I'm innocent."

"You sent the soldiers because you want our diamonds!" the teacher said.

"Don't blame all wazungu for the crimes of a few," Bondo said. He owned one of the three stationery shops in town. His son was an altar boy.

"Let's go," the nun said, tugging at the father. "You'll bleed to death if they don't fix that wound soon."

"I didn't send them," Father Stephen said. "You are my people. You are my children. How could I hurt you?"

"Hypocrite!" the teacher shouted.

"Don't mind him, Father," the mayor said. "They killed all his children and his wife. It's the grief making him say such things."

"We are all aggrieved," Bondo said again. "But does that mean that we should blame all wazungu for the crimes of a few? We know about the mines, and we know why this war started, but blaming Father Stephen for it is sheer stupidity."

"You are the stupid one," the teacher said. "This fat mzungu is a thief! When he came he was so thin that the wind could have blown him away, but now see how fat he has become! He's stealing our wealth!"

"Father," the nun was saying, tugging at his frock. "Let's go to the clinic."

"I'm not a thief!" Father Stephen shouted. Blood ran down his face. He wavered, as though about to fall.

"Please go to the clinic," the mayor said. "The reverend will manage the service. Thank you for coming by, but please leave now."

"I'm not a thief," Father Stephen said.

"The teacher has a point," Timeo said. He was a carpenter. He got married hardly a month ago. His wife was with Kera's mother when the soldiers came. She was pregnant. "Why didn't they attack your church?"

"This is madness," the mayor said.

"How do you know the Catholic church is the only building they didn't shoot at?" Bondo said.

"We searched all houses looking for victims," Timeo said. "The Catholic church was untouched."

A hush fell upon the graveyard. Even the wind seemed to stop, and the leaves fell silent, as though to fuel the accusation. Kera heard a twig break as the carpenter took a step toward the wazungu. Father Stephen's mouth hung ajar, saliva dropping onto his garb.

"Many other buildings are untouched," Baba said. Everyone turned to him. "They didn't attack the Social Centre or the headmaster's house."

"But they killed the headmaster," the teacher said. "They wounded Agira. He may not survive the day." Agira was the caretaker of the Social Centre. After the English had gone, the complex had been poorly maintained. The golf course was overgrown, the swimming pool had not had water for decades, and bats infested the cinema.

"Please," the reverend said. "Let's not behave like the soldiers. Vengeance is for the Lord. I lost my family. I'm grieved. But we've no proof that Father Steven is working with soldiers. No proof at all."

Kera could feel the tension thaw. Sound returned to the world. The wind resumed blowing, the leaves sang, and a murmur spread through the crowd.

"Thank you," Father Stephen said in a weak whisper, finally letting the nuns take him away.

"Don't let them go!" the teacher screamed, fighting the men holding him. "Beat them! Kill them!"

But the crowd parted to allow Father Stephen to retreat to his car.

## :: Chapter 3 ::

Kera fell into bed early that night. Though nightmares beset his dreams, he did not awaken until late the next day when a ray of sunlight fell in from his window and burnt through his eyelids. He had a headache. They lived in Chandi. It was not a slum anymore, but it still had a high population density. Every morning he awoke to a cacophony. Women gossiping to each other across the yard, laughing, infants screaming for attention, children playing, the screech of a broom sweeping a compound, the ring of aluminium clashing as young girls washed pans and dishes, the caw of crows.

Life.

But that morning he did not hear any noise. For several moments he could not tell where he was. Then it all came back with such force that he felt a sharp pain in his heart. There were two other beds in the room, both unmade, as they had been the previous day when Okee and Acii had crept out of sleep. Even now it seemed as though they had just walked out, leaving the sheets scattered all over the floor. He watched the dust motes floating on sunbeams and tears wet the pillow.

*Bring them back to life*, he prayed to Baba.

An aroma wafted in from the kitchen. It stirred hunger to bubble in his stomach. A sizzling sound tickled his saliva. He drooled onto the pillow, and it mixed with tears. Was it Baba cooking, or had he brought Mama back to life?

Kera scrambled out of bed. The door opened into a short corridor, which had four other doors. One led to the master bedroom, another to the bathroom. Both were closed. The one immediately to his left was ajar. It led to the living room. Kera saw the teacher on a sofa, reading a dog-eared history book. There were two other people with him, but Kera could see only their legs. The fourth door, at the opposite end of the corridor, led to the kitchen. It stood wide open, letting in smoke. If it were Mama cooking, there would not have been so much smoke. He found Baba, still wearing the goggles, straddled over the charcoal stove.

"How have you woken up?" Baba greeted, without turning around.

"I woke up fine," he replied. His voice a croak, barely a whisper.

"Today I'll build a solar-powered stove," Baba said, turning an omelette in the pan. "I hate smoke."

*You could simply bring Mama back to life*, Kera thought, and Baba finally turned to face him. His face had grown a shade darker.

"Sit." Baba pointed at a three-legged stool.

Kera sat. Baba scooped the omelette out of the pan, put it on a plate on top of four other omelettes, and put a kettle on the stove. Without asking, Kera took a slice of bread smeared with odi and wolfed it down. The taste reminded him of Mama. She made him odi whenever he left for another term in boarding school after he had complained to her that they ate nothing but boiled beans and posho. He mixed odi in beans to give it a better taste and gain supplementary nutrients from the groundnuts and simsim in the paste. The memories caused something cold to run down his cheeks. He wiped it away quickly.

Baba sat on a stool beside him.

"I can bring her back to life," Baba said. "But I won't. Whatever goes to the other side is not meant to come back. Mama, Okee, Acii, they have gone over. Are they in a better place or is it a worse-off place? I don't know. But it's now their home. Bringing them will only unleash evil."

Kera ran out through the back door into the backyard, which they shared with five other families. Laundry fluttered on a wire. A neighbour had washed clothes the previous dawn just before the soldiers came. Behind the laundry stood a small building, which was meant to be a store, but which Karama lived in. Kera sat down on the doorsteps, buried his face in his palms, and allowed himself to cry.

Nearly half an hour later, Baba brought him breakfast. A mug of milk, slices of bread smeared with odi, and an omelet. Kera wiped his eyes and ate. Baba went back in without saying a word. After the meal Kera took the dishes into the kitchen and caught a quarrel coming from the living room.

"Our gods have woken up," the teacher was saying. "They want us to finish off the mzungu."

"Our gods are more just than that," the mayor said.

"If we kill innocent blood, then we are no different from them," the reverend said.

"It's time to revenge," the teacher said.

"Vengeance serves no purpose," Baba said. "I called you to talk about the gift our ancestors gave me and how we can use it to defend ourselves. I don't want to talk about vengeance and bloodshed."

*Ancestors?* Kera frowned. Baba had insisted that the hissing creatures were not spirits or gods, just people. A different kind of people. Why then was he telling these men that they were spirits? Was it to protect the secret?

"We can't defend ourselves without weapons," the teacher said.

"Even if I wanted to, I can't design weapons," Baba said. "The spirits that possessed me are not warriors. They won't allow me to create things that will end up killing people."

"What ancestors are those?" the teacher said. "Our ancestors were not cowards. They fought the British. They resisted colonisation."

"Well, I can't build weapons," Baba said.

"But we need to kill those who try to kill us," the teacher said.

"Weapons are the reason our world is a bad place," the reverend said.

"And you think you will just wish away the badness?" the teacher said. "Get real. Without weapons we won't be able to defend ourselves. Never."

"Yes, we can," Baba said. "I can build a wall so high and

so thick and so strong that not even a tank will bring it down. I can create a moat of fire outside this wall, a fire that will never go out."

"You talk like a madman," the teacher said.

"We've seen his machine," the mayor said. "He can do it if he says he can."

Kera crept away. He wandered about in the empty streets. Even the birds seemed to be staying away from the town. The scars of the massacre glared at him. Burnt vehicles, shattered buildings, blood stains on the pavement. On Main Street he saw a family making their way out of town with a few possessions on bicycles. *The stupid ones*, Kera thought.

Katong had been the safest place before the attack. Leaving it would be jumping from the frying pan into the fire. If Baba built the wall and fire moat, would they be safe? Probably, but not from artillery fire. The streets had too many painful memories, so he escaped to the workshop, which evoked only metallic memories.

Baba never put a padlock on the outer gate. The yard had nothing valuable, only scrap and immovable tools. He locked the shop, however, for it contained merchandise, household utensils, iron furniture, and he kept valuable tools in a backroom. But that day Kera found a padlock on the outer gate, an expensive type that used a combination like a safe.

He stared at the padlock for a long moment, then climbed over the gate, and jumped into the workshop. He found two machines that Baba must have made in the night. One looked like a chair with a wheel. Baba had cannibalised the wheel from an old green bicycle of Kera, which he had meant to repair and give to Okee. The chair, crafted out of iron and cushioned with red leather and sponge, had been Baba's favourite, a piece of art that Kera's grandfather had made many years ago. Just under the seat was a black box made entirely out of the strange glass rock. Two large sheets of leather were attached to the back of the chair. In front of the chair were a handlebar and gear box. Kera puzzled over the machine until he spread out the leather and the purpose struck him. Wings.

*I can build a flying machine.*

The second object was a rod twice the length of his arm and just as thick with four slide switches at the back. It had a slot at the top with a mirror inside. When he looked into the open end of the tube, he saw a row of mirrors made from the strange glass rock, placed delicately one behind the other, and each caught the image of his eye.

He slid the switches from one position to another. Nothing happened. He left the rod on the table, where he had found it, and crawled into the corpse of a van. He sat behind the wheel, and memories of his lost family saddened him.

The sun was high in the sky when Baba came in alone, still wearing the welding goggles. Kera thought his skin had again grown several shades darker and now looked as though smeared with grease. He gave Kera a smile and spoke as he strode to his worktable.

"Good you are here," Baba said. "Have you seen that thing?"

"The flying machine?" Kera said, but stayed in the van.

Baba climbed onto the chair and pulled a lever. A pair of six-foot wings spread out. He peddled. A whirr filled the workshop. The machine did not move. A stand prevented the wheel from touching the ground. He peddled harder, and the wheel spanned in a blur of motion. Baba kicked away the stand, and the machine jumped into the air. Kera gaped. In spite of all he had seen Baba do, he had not imagined that the chair would fly. The wings flapping like that of a bird. Baba stayed only a few feet above the ground within the covers of the wall. He later told Kera it was because he did not want anyone else to see the flying machine. He circled about for a minute and landed.

"I call it a bruka," Baba said, laughing. "Do you want to give it a try?"

Kera's face tightened. He had just buried Mama, Acii, and Okee. Laughing did not feel right, and certainly flying for pleasure was immoral.

"It's just like riding a bicycle," Baba said. "Give it a try."

Kera shook his head.

"I built it for you," Baba said.

Kera did not reply. He could not bear the weight of Baba's stare. He looked away. He felt more than he heard Baba approach. A strong perfume filled his nose. The smell grew stronger as Baba came closer. Kera turned to him in puzzlement. Baba never used any cosmetics, not even Vaseline, but now he had applied a greasy ointment. It made his skin darker, and it gave him a strong, flowery scent.

Kera looked away at the rusted wheel, at a spider web on the dashboard. His vision blurred.

"I wish I could also cry," Baba said. "I wish tears could roll down my face. But the rock people touched me. I can't sleep. I can't get tired. I can't eat. I pretend to eat in public, but I don't need food anymore. And the sun burns my skin."

*You died*, Kera wept silently. *You died in the cave.*

Baba put a hand on his shoulder. It felt like ice. Kera cringed away.

"I'm not dead," Baba said. "I'm only different."

Kera could still not understand. Baba surely had not forgotten Mama's laughter or how she sang as she ground simsim into odi or Acii's laughter or how Okee loved to chase after lizards. How could he remember them and not grieve?

"You still have Karama," Baba said. "You can rescue him before he turns into a monster. I could have done it myself, but these changes," he paused. "I can't see faraway things. I can't ask anyone else to do it, for I don't want them to know about the flash gun."

Kera stared at the cobweb, at a trapped insect wing glimmering in a drop of sunlight. A cloud swept in, and the wing lost its glow to become just a shrivelled thing with torn edges. He heard Baba sigh and walk away. He looked up to see Baba standing beside the rod on the table, arms akimbo, head slightly bowed, maybe thinking about destroying it.

Kera thought about the flying machine and the rod—the flash gun—for the rest of the day, wondering how a weepy boy of sixteen could rescue an elder brother from an army of savages. He had been eight the last time he had engaged in a fight when a girl had beaten him up for stealing her mango. Karama was the tougher one, with muscles that gave him the nickname Schwarzenegger Commando. If their situations were reversed, with Kera the hostage, Karama would not have hesitated to jump into Baba's flying machine and ride away to rescue his little brother.

But he could not do it.

How could he?

:::

He woke up the next morning from another night of ceaseless nightmares to find Baba had prepared him breakfast, but no sign of Baba. As he ate, he noticed a candle holder shaped like a dove on the kitchen table. A week before the attack Mama had asked Baba to make her one for the clay holders she had kept breaking. She had pestered him for it, and Baba had kept giving her excuses until the night before the attack when she asked Kera if he had learnt enough to craft her one. Kera had only smiled in shyness. The dove was warm, and he thought it had Mama's scent. Fighting back tears, he dropped it and ran to the workshop, where he found Baba making another candle holder.

"What do you want me to do?" he said, trying hard not to sniffle.

Baba gave him a quick smile, went into the room behind the shop, and returned with the rod.

"Did you see this?" Baba said.

"Is that the flash gun?" Kera said.

Baba fished a sliver of glass from his pocket and slid it into a slot on top of the rod.

"It's the safety," Baba said. "Without it the weapon is useless. Do you know what the sun is made of?"

"Fire?"

"Yes. Fire."

Baba picked an empty tin of paint from a waste bin and put it on the roof of the van. He then stood several paces away and took aim. Kera waited for a bang, for something spectacular. Nothing happened. He turned to his father with a questioning look. In that instant he heard a faint sizzling. He turned back to the tin. It had vanished. A whiff of blue smoke wafted lazily, then thinned out into oblivion.

"You can't see it in daylight," Baba said. "If it were night, you would've seen a bluish light."

Baba opened a chamber at the back to reveal rechargeable AA alkaline batteries. "See? I modified these so they use solar energy to produce a fire so hot that it can punch a hole through a mountain. If you have the patience you can make the mountain disappear inch by inch."

*Heat ray*, Kera thought, recalling his favourite book, *The War of the Worlds*. He wondered if the hissing creature was an alien. Some theories had it that human beings originated from outer space, hence their inability to live at peace with the environment. Maybe these aliens found Earth inhospitable because of the sun, so they lived inside caves. Maybe they inhabited apes to survive, and the symbiotic relationship gave birth to humans.

"They are not aliens," Baba said, using the English word since he could not find an equivalent in Luo.

Baba pulled out a strange pair of goggles from a drawer. It had two miniature tubes on the glass, one for each eye. He turned a dial, and the tubes elongated with the whir of a zoom lens.

"If you wear this at the top of a mountain," Baba said, "you'll see ants walking at the foot of the mountain. With this and the flash gun, you can wipe out an entire army without them knowing what hit them. So you see, the mission will be easy and safe. You stay in the sky all the time and vaporise the soldiers one at a time. When they are all dead, you fly down and bring your brother back home."

That night the nightmares did not come. Instead, Kera had vivid dreams of Kibuuka, a warrior who could fly like a bird and shoot arrows at the enemy, and of Luanda Magere, another invincible warrior who was made out of stone. In the dream Kera was a superhero with the combined ability of Kibuuka and Luanda Magere. He got flying power from his mother, who in the dream lived in the moon, and he got his stone flesh from his father, who lived in a dark cave just outside their home. He darted about the sky, unleashing lightning onto the warlords, putting an end to wanton rape and murder and all the evils that the war had brought upon his country. The dream was so vivid that, for several moments when he woke up, he could not remember who he was.

*Are you ready?* Baba said.

The voice added to Kera's confusion, for he was alone in the room. Kera stepped out of bed and got dressed up quickly. As he zipped up his jeans, Baba appeared at the doorway with the eternal smile. He waved a lunch box.

"I packed you something to eat," Baba said.

"Thank you," Kera said. "How did you sleep?" he added in greeting. Only after he had said it did he remember that Baba was not capable of sleep anymore. He wondered if he should have instead used the simpler English greeting "Good Morning" or the Swahili "Habari za asubuhior." Still Baba replied.

"I slept well. Maybe you?"

"I slept well, too."

It was still dark when they got to the workshop. Baba had already packed the bruka in a red box fitted with wheels. Kera rolled it out of the workshop and out of town into the valley. It was no heavier than a bicycle. He would learn to fly it and shoot the flash gun, but the project had to remain a secret for Baba was in a moral quandary. Kera understood his argument: if human beings had not invented weapons, the world would be a much safer place. Fistfights were savage and bestial, but surely not as apocalyptic as automatic rifles and atomic bombs. No one had to know about the flash gun.

Shortly after he left the workshop, ten men, including the teacher, the mayor, and the reverend, arrived. He could not identify all of them in the half-lights, but Baba had told him who would come. They would help build a giant machine to construct a wall and fire moat around the town. They saw Kera pushing the red box up the street, but he was too far away for them to check its contents. Several people clearing debris from the streets cast Kera curious glances but did not ask questions.

In the valley he followed the stream eastward until he was four miles away from the town, where he could hope for privacy. He waited until the sun was up before he took to the air. The first time he flew, vertigo attacked him. He went just above the trees and nearly crashed in panic. He overcame this fear and went higher. As Baba had said, it was just like riding a bicycle in the air. The tricky bit was getting the gear lever right. Just under the handlebars Baba had modified the car gear box. One took the craft up. Two took it down. Three was for hovering. Four fixed the flight horizontally and allowed the craft to run on the ground. Baba called five the autopilot. It enabled the craft to move in a straight line without the rider steering or peddling. Six put the craft in reverse. Seven caused an umbrella-like parachute to pop out in a crisis to ensure safe landing. Baba had provided a helmet to enable him to breathe in the slipstream and wear the telescopic goggles.

For three days he practiced. He left home before dawn and returned after sunset, hiding the bruka in a cave to preserve its secret. The more comfortable he became in the air, the more he dreamed of Kibuuka and Luanda Magere conjoined to form the flying man of stone. When he slept at night and took naps during the day, the dreams came with such vividness that he could not be sure they were dreams anymore. He came to believe they were trips he took to another world, where spirits prepared him to save, not just his brother, but the entire country.

After three days he flew as comfortably as an eagle. He would soar until he was no more than a speck in the sky, then engage the hover gear and shoot at targets on the ground. The telescopic goggles enabled him to see rats in the fields, even from the height of a mountain peak. The flash gun vaporised the targets with pinpoint accuracy. At first, he would burn a hole into the ground after hitting a rat, but he learnt how to do it properly. By adjusting the circumference of the rays, he could drill only a tiny hole in the rat's head to kill it.

He loved to watch the town from the sky, loved to admire the rooftops of Chandi. It looked like a graveyard of many childhoods. Dolls, toys, bicycle tyres, shoes, bits and pieces of children's things had found their way onto the roofs. A red leather ball, which the sun had bleached to pale pink, had been a birthday gift from Baba when Kera turned ten. It had made him the most popular boy in the neighbourhood. Before that they had only played with balls made of polythene bags or banana fibres. This one was leather and inflatable. For months it had bounced up and down the street, flew over trees in the valley, struck rocks, and bounced off the stream. It had broken many windows and earned many boys a thrashing. He could not remember how it ended up on the roof. They must have gotten bored of the imported toy and resumed playing with their homemade gadgets.

In those three days Baba built a wall around the town a hundred feet high, twelve feet thick, and a moat of fire twenty feet wide. Machines replicated gas, which fed the fire with an inexhaustible supply of fuel. There were two gates, one in the west facing the city, the other in the east facing the mineral-rich northeastern region. Since Baba had refused to make a machine to provide an inexhaustible supply of food, the gates opened every morning to let farmers out and let them back in every noon.

The miracle wall gave the teacher fame and power, as Baba refused to take public credit for the town's defences. Even the handful of men who helped him build the machines did not know who really was behind it. While the mayor and reverend welcomed the idea, for it kept the town safe, their Christian minds associated it with ancestral spirit worship, hence devil worship, so they did not openly condone the miracle wall. Thus the teacher gained a springboard.

"Our gods have woken up," he told the town. "They've been asleep all these years as foreign gods laid our land to waste and turned us into slaves, but now they've woken up. They heard our cries. They saw our suffering. They know we are tired of wars and famine so they've come to our rescue."

The teacher became a priest. A messiah. A prophet. A few people gathered at his home every evening to worship, but most of the townfolk, though they acknowledged his new status as a spiritual leader, were Christians. Once the wall was up, the Anglicans asked the reverend to pray to rid it of demonic power and bless it with the blood of Jesus Christ. The teacher attended the service. Just before the reverend's sermon, he gave a speech imploring the town to abandon Christianity and return to the religion of their forefathers. When the Catholics asked Father Steven to hold a similar service and sprinkle holy water on the wall in a purification ritual, the teacher blew up. His followers disrupted the service, smashing windows and statues. Once again the teacher beat up Father Steven.

"I have no problem with an African priest leading the prayers," the teacher told the congregation. "But I'll not allow these wazungu to steal our powers! Never!"

The night after the incident the mayor came to see Baba.

"I'm worried about the teacher," the mayor said. "I don't like his actions at all."

They were eating supper, which Baba had prepared, boiled potatoes and chicken. It tasted like nothing Mama ever cooked, but hunger made Kera wolf it all down and lick his fingers.

"I would have no problem if it was just a case of Christianity versus African religions," the mayor said. "But this man is preaching hatred against wazungu."

"What do you want me to do?" Baba said.

"Stop him," the mayor said. "He claims the ancestors have chosen him, but if people knew it's actually you who was blessed, they won't listen to him."

"No."

"Why not?"

"You do it. You are the mayor. You are the politician."

"I'm also a Christian."

"So?"

"People listen to the teacher because all along he has preached against Christianity and all kizungu things. They won't listen to me if I told them the ancestors are speaking through me. But you, if you showed people your eyes, they'd believe you."

"I can't do it."

"Why not? You've got to stop the hatred."

"I've never been a political person," Baba said. "All I ever did was work metals. But you are the mayor, and what you are asking me to do is actually your responsibility. You. The reverend. The other leaders. You can convince the town to embrace the new gods without embracing racism."

Kera licked his plate dry, left them arguing, went to his bedroom, and fell fast asleep. He wandered again that night into the world of superheroes, where he flew with Kibuuka and fought beside Luanda Magere. He dreamed of Mama, too, that she had prepared malakwang and they were eating together as a family in those happy days before the soldiers came. He woke up to find Baba sitting on one of the other beds, watching him.

"How did you sleep?" Baba said.

"Fine," Kera said, sitting up, pulling the bedclothes to cover his nakedness.

"I'll tell you where they are holding Karama," Baba said.

Kera looked up, wondering about the hoarseness in Baba's voice. Only then did he notice that Baba's skin was peeling off.

"I'm dying," Baba said.

"No," Kera said.

"The sun," Baba said. "It's killing me. I have to go to a place of total darkness."

*Like the hissing creatures*, Kera thought. *He is becoming one of them. Please, no.*

"You have Karama," Baba said. "Rescue him, and then I'll destroy that gun. I can't leave it behind. You can stay with the bruka."

Kera felt something cold running down his face. He hated himself at that moment. How could he ever be Kibuuka? How could he ever be Luanda Magere if his tears came as easily as that of a little girl? He buried his face into his palms to hide his shame, but that did not stop the pain that wrecked his heart.

"I don't want to leave you," Baba said. "But the sun will kill me if I stay."

## :: Chapter 4 ::

Rage propelled him through the sky. The chill bit into his face. His fingers froze on the handlebars. Behind him the horizon reddened with the waking sun. He flew over the valley of spirits, over the vast swamp, going west, away from home, away from his dying father.

If he failed to save Karama, he would not have anyone left. He would be all alone in the world, just a little weepy boy playing the superhero. Doubts beset him. Attacking during the day, rather than in the night when the gun's flashes might warn the soldiers, had sounded like a good idea. The flash was invisible in daylight, and the gun made no noise. So theoretically, he could kill all the soldiers before they realised what was happening. Yet soldiers would see their comrades falling dead or vanishing into thin air if he used a wider flash circumference. They were not fools. They would know something was up. They would hide. And then what? Would they sit back like ducks and watch as he took them out one at a time? Some warlords had attack helicopters and anti-aircraft guns. What if someone spotted him in the sky and fired?

Fear fanned his anger. The realisation that he would not save his brother flooded his mouth with the taste of rotten milk. He would soon be all alone. Baba was turning into a shadow. He had a machine that would dig a hole in the bedroom, tunnel under the town, and then into the valley where he would join the hissing creatures. There would be no grave, just a hole under the bed. They still had some days, five at most, Baba had said, and then Kera would have no one left.

Unless he saved Karama.

Villages and small towns appeared far below him. Burnt huts, bombed-out buildings, vehicles upturned on the roadsides. Yet, amidst the wounds, life bustled. People crept out of their huts armed with hoes or jerry cans as they went to draw water. He flew over the ruins of a trading centre. Two men staggered out of a bar. It had a makeshift roof, no windows, no door, and its walls were black from a fire. Kera could not hear the drunks, but he could see them singing, dancing, falling on the road, and laughing. An old woman swept the front yard, empty clay pots and beer straws were scattered around her.

Shortly after passing the ruined town, he came upon a bunch of soldiers. There were ten of them on foot patrol. They had stopped four women, two of whom had babies on their backs, one had a suitcase, another had a bundle of clothing. *Refugees*, Kera thought, *in search of a mythically peaceful land*. One soldier used a knife to rip off one woman's dress. She dropped her luggage and tried to cling onto her dress to cover her nakedness. Kera thought she was screaming, as the other women begged, as the infants wailed, and as the other soldiers cheered. The soldier's knife slashed and slashed, leaving the woman stark naked.

Kera engaged Gear Three. The bruka went into hover mode. He pulled the ray gun from under the seat just as the soldier threw the naked woman onto the ground. He could use a wider ray circumference to vaporise the boy, but that would take several seconds as opposed to a bullet hole-sized circumference, which would happen in a split second.

He turned a dial on his goggles. It zoomed in until he could count the pimples on the soldier's face—a boy, about his own age, eyes red with flames of alcohol. Maybe this pimple-infested goon had thrown the grenade that ripped Mama to bits. Maybe his gun ripped little Acii and Okee. Maybe he had raped dozens of women old enough to be his grandmother. Kera thumbed the trigger. The boy fell dead beside the woman. The other soldiers laughed, maybe thinking it an antic, until the blood flowed out of the boy's head onto the tarmac.

One soldier stepped closer to examine the dead boy's head. Kera shot him. The others broke into a run, jumping for cover into the drainage ditch at the roadside. Kera swung the gun from one to the other, thinking he was too slow, but a slight press of his thumb was all it took for the gun to flash. One by one, he killed them all.

The women were flat on the road. Kera wanted to go down to them, to comfort them, the way he had not comforted his mother. He could not, but he could show them where to go. So he burned holes and lines on the road, drawing an arrow pointing east, and spelling out the name of his town. Katong.

One woman stood up. She looked about in confusion, at the bodies, at the blood flowing down the gray tarmac, and then at the writing on the road. Kera hoped she could read.

Only when he resumed flight did he hear the pounding of his heart. His fingers trembled. Unable to concentrate on steering the craft, the flight became bumpy, as though he were driving fast over a potholed road. He set the ornithopter to autopilot and let the emotions wash over him. He had just snuffed out the life of ten people—ten boys—who in another world might have played football with him, maybe grazed goats with him—boys who were ripped away from their parents and turned into monsters. He had punched holes into their heads just as he had done the rats he used for target practice. Did that not make him a monster, too? Maybe their mothers were still alive somewhere, praying for their safe return home. Maybe they had little Aciis and Okees who were waiting for them.

Kera felt faint. Tears blurred his vision. He engaged the hover gear and cried out for the first time since he was ten. He wailed for a long time. The sun rode higher into the sky. The day became warmer. He was numbed, unable to go forward, unable to go back.

Then he saw smoke on the ground, in the horizon, black fumes over the trees. He zoomed in on it and saw a village burning. There were corpses on the ground, some hacked to pieces, others riddled with bullets. No sign of the perpetrators. He scanned the bushes, the road running from the village. He saw whiffs of dust in the air. A car had just passed by. He followed the dust and caught a pickup speeding away with a machine gun on its back, a dozen soldiers crammed beneath the gun. Blood dripped from their machetes.

He pulled out his gun and aimed at the soldiers. One of them, whose nascent moustache was smeared with blood, had a frown on his face. Kera moved his gun to the next one, but these soldiers were not cheering as the foot patrol had. The blank expressions probably indicated that they had derived no joy in their deed. Before he could make a decision, the car plunged into a forest and vanished from his sight.

He took off the telescopic goggles. He thought he would resume crying, that grief would overwhelm him. Yet, all he felt was a tightening in his stomach. He clenched the handlebars, teeth grinding.

"You are the flying man of stone," a voice whispered, in such a low tone that it could have been the wind singing to him. He looked over his shoulder, expecting to see someone standing on a cloud behind the bruka. Nothing.

"You are Kibuuka," the voice continued. "You are Luanda Magere." He now thought it belonged to his mother. "You are the salvation of your people."

"Ma," he said. It came out a weak whisper.

The voice did not speak again.

He searched the clouds. Only then did the surreal morning strike him. It was something straight out of a dream. Maybe it was all a dream, and anytime now Mama would awaken him and give him a mug of hot porridge and a bowl of roasted njugu.

"Ma," he said again, a little louder. "Is that you?"

The clouds did not answer. They did not open up to reveal the gods within them. They sailed by in silence, lazily, on their way to make rain and bless the ground.

Kera felt strangely at peace. The miasma of guilt vanished. He was the flying man of stone. He had just saved four women and two children from rape and death. Why should he feel bad about it? The world lay in ruins. A war raged, filling the rivers with blood and choking the swamps with corpses. The streets bled, homes burned down, dreams turned to ash, and misery flowed in the veins of the people. They needed a god to fight for them. He could be that god, just like Kibuuka and Luanda Magere. He could bring peace back to the land.

Kera donned the goggles and resumed flight.

He sped after the pickup, eager to vaporise the murderers. He did not see it again. Instead, he came upon Kapeto Army Barracks, a sprawling complex of circular huts built in a dozen rings around a three-storied brick structure.

The warlord lived in that brick building. A flag waved on its roof. About two hundred meters north of the barracks was a separate ring of huts encircling hundreds of wooden cages, each about ten square feet with about a score of prisoners. His brother was somewhere in one of those coops.

Kera zoomed in. The prisoners were eating porridge, which seemed nothing more than dirty water. From their gaunt faces he thought they were probably starving. Maybe the thin porridge was all they ever ate. In a clearing at the edge of the prison, some of the male captives, cuddling wooden guns, stood in four lines in front of three soldiers. *Recruits*, Kera thought, *out for training*. He guessed that those in the cages had not yet yielded. Most bore the signs of beating, eyes swollen shut, bloated faces, torn lips, broken noses.

He searched from cage to cage, aware of the futility of his mission, for many people were face down, maybe unconscious, maybe dead. When he found Karama, after nearly an hour of searching, he failed to recognise him for a few moments. A bandage wrapped half of Karama's face, covering up one eye. Blood had soaked through the bandage, a smudge where the eye should have been. Had he lost his eye? Would Baba invent a machine to cure him?

Even though Baba's dreaded machines could clone life or generate food or heal, he would do nothing if he saw Karama's face. He would simply say, "Your brother is back. Look after each other," and then vanish into that dark world inside of rocks.

A soldier stood beside Karama's cage. He had streaks of gray in his hair, wrinkled skin, and a faded green uniform with tattered seams. A rusty AK-47 hung on his back from a sisal rope. His hands trembled as he filled mugs with porridge, probably a sign that he drank too much alcohol. The prisoners accepted the meal, seemingly without complaint or thanks. This soldier would be the first to die in the rescue mission. Kera's thumb hovered above the trigger button. He could not shoot. The old man was not doing any harm and probably had never hurt anyone. He was only feeding prisoners.

Kera instead turned the flash gun onto the frames of the cage and pressed, vaporising wood. One side fell open. The prisoners scrambled away in confusion. The old soldier dropped the serving jug, splashing porridge, and snatched his gun. He cocked it but did not shoot. He did not even point it at the prisoners. He stepped away from the cage, confused, and shouted something.

Kera's goggles zoomed out to gain a wider field of vision. Three soldiers were running to the cage. Kera thought he heard the clank of metal as they cocked their guns, but it was only in his head. He could not hear anything. He was watching a silent movie.

A soldier with sergeant's stripes inspected the cage. He took out his pistol and pointed it at a prisoner, a man with a bald head. The sergeant asked a question. The bald man shrugged. The gun flashed. A cloud of red exploded from the bald head, splashing the people closest to him. The prisoners dropped their mugs and scrambled away from the sergeant, screaming. They had nowhere to run. The sergeant turned his gun on another prisoner.

Kera's gun flashed.

It was easier when he thought of it as *Shooter*, a video game he used to play at school.

The sergeant dropped. His finger pressed the trigger as he fell. The bullet hit the soldier standing beside him. Again Kera saw an explosion of red.

Other soldiers opened fire, shooting randomly at unseen enemies and the prisoners, who fell flat inside their cages. Kera fired and fired, aware that he was too slow, dropping one soldier after another. Panic spread through the camp. Soldiers ran toward Karama's cage in confusion. Some took cover behind whatever shelter they could find— wheelbarrows, boulders.

Karama and other prisoners slipped out of the cage and took cover beneath it.

"Run!" Kera screamed, but they could not hear him.

He cut open more cages. Prisoners scrambled out. Some were bold enough to pick up the guns the soldiers had dropped. Now they shot at the uniformed men. The battle intensified. Not once did anyone look up into the sky. Even if they did, they would not have seen Kera. He was just a speck in the sky with the sun behind him. His gun flashed and flashed—invisible rays, one at a time, searching for men in green, punching holes into their heads, just as the virtual gun had searched for bad guys in *Shooter*, searching for wooden bars and vaporising them to free prisoners.

It seemed like an hour had passed. It was probably just a few minute. He had killed many of the soldiers inside the prison. The rest were hiding out of his sight. Tanks and armoured cars were racing from the main barracks as a host of soldiers ran to the front line. Kera turned his gun on the vehicles, ripping tanks apart, slicing machine guns off armoured cars, vaporising engines, turning them to scrap.

But the foot soldiers were closing in on the prison. If they went in, there would be too many of them. Kera would not be able to stop a massacre, but he could stop them from reaching the prison. He cut a ditch in front of them, moving his gun slowly over the ground, keeping the trigger pressed down. The ditch formed steadily, but too slowly. He wished he could do it faster, but even then it had an effect.

Soldiers saw the ground opening up in front of them— no fire, no earthquake, no digging, just a ditch twenty feet deep suddenly appearing, growing longer and longer. They dropped their guns and fled, only to face fire from their commanders anxious to stop a mass desertion.

Artillery fired, distracting him from the ditch. The shell fell inside the prison. Kera heard the boom. The explosion sent prisoners scampering, trying to get out, but getting out meant passing a ring of sandbags and machine guns that ripped them apart. Kera was torn. He could not take out the artillery and the machine guns at the same time. Tears spat afresh, clouding his vision. He was no superman. He could not fight a whole army. His super gun could only kill one soldier at a time. He was not fast enough to stop the massacre.

More shells fell in the prison. He turned to the artillery, a row of six guns. He fired. Nothing. The battery was dead. He ejected it, popped in another. He cut the artillery into pieces. Soldiers watched in horror as the big guns broke up in front of them. Then Kera turned to the machine guns. He took out one at a time. Too bad his gun was silent. If it made noise, maybe it would tell the soldiers where he was. Then they would stop shooting at the prisoners.

All of a sudden, the soldiers abandoned the sandbags and fled. Maybe they had finally realised that a ghost was killing them. Their flight enabled the prisoners to get out. Beyond the prison were open fields, a bush, and a forest. Many prisoners headed for the forest, seeing it would give them better cover.

Seeing that the massacre had ceased and many prisoners now had guns and were fighting off the few soldiers remaining in the prison, Kera spent a few moments etching a message onto the trunk of several trees. Just one word. "Katong." It was difficult work and drained two batteries, but he created enough messages scattered over a wide area. He hoped the prisoners would get it and head for Katong. Kera could not be in all places at the same time, but if there were as many people as possible within the walls of his town, it would be easier for him to protect them.

Still he thought he could instill fear into the soldiers. They would surely be talking about the mysterious attack, and they would attribute it to ghosts and spirits. He could stress the point and play on their beliefs. Then maybe it would stop them from harming civilians.

He vaporised the three-storied building, hoping the warlord was inside. The soldiers watched in horror as the building vanished from their sight. He left only one wall standing, on which he wrote, "Stop Hurting Our People," in Swahili. A small crowd quickly gathered to read the message.

Only then did he remember the mission. Karama. He turned back to the prison. He could not remember where Karama's cage had been. The prison had turned into a mess. There were many unopened cages. Kera cut them loose as he continued to search for his brother. He tried to work as fast as he could. His wrist hurt, his thumb ached. He ejected the sixth battery and popped in another. He hoped Karama was among those who had already made it to the forest, but he had to be sure. After he had opened every cage, he searched the dead and those too wounded to move.

He found Karama. A large part of his head was missing.

## :: Chapter 5 ::

He thought grief would rip him apart. He thought he would disintegrate. But the death of his brother only left him with a sense of disappointment. They had not been close. With five years between them, they never had much in common. They did not share friends or play games together. They did not even share the same roof, for as long as Kera could remember, Karama had lived in the little building out in the backyard. He could not remember ever having a one-on-one conversation with Karama. They had never even fought before.

For nearly ten minutes Kera watched blood flow from Karama's head. He had uncles, aunts, and cousins who he could look to for family support, but none lived in town. They had not seen or heard from any of them since the war broke out.

His vision blurred. He wiped tears away and forced his eyes off the carnage. Soldiers still ran about in their barracks in utter confusion. Some had jumped into vehicles and were speeding away. Hopefully, they would spread word of the terror that had befallen their barracks. The prisoners had escaped. Kera was glad to see some reading a sign he had etched on a tree trunk. It warmed his heart to see them heading eastwards toward Katong.

*Salvation*, Kera thought. He had failed to save Karama, but he could still bring sanity back to the world. He needed the flash gun. He could not let Baba destroy it.

He believed human beings were a cross between the alien hissing creature and apes, that human consciousness and intelligence came from these aliens. Maybe, seeing how humans used this intelligence to ruin the world, they forbade Baba from revealing any knowledge other than what was necessary to protect the valley. But Baba, or the human bit of him still left, had created a supergun to rescue his son.

Kera had failed him. Now Baba would want to destroy the gun. He would argue that the world was better off without it. Yet, Kera had experienced its magic. He had saved four women from rape and possibly death. He had destroyed a warlord's barracks and saved thousands of people from being turned into zombies ready to kill, rape, and maim for the love of minerals and the illusion of power. With the flash gun he was Kibuuka and Luanda Magere. He could instill fear in warlords and bring back peace.

He spent the day in the skies, floating, mourning, letting the chill kiss his skin, feeling the wind in his wings and the weight of grief in his heart. When hungry, he ate roasted potatoes and chicken, which Baba had wrapped in banana leaves. He did not zoom in on the details on the ground, for that would make him more miserable. He instead kept the goggles at their widest angle, giving him panoramic views of hills, of rivers flowing through the green, red dirt roads and gray tarmac roads cutting through the lush vegetation. He stayed up there until the sun started to descend.

He did not keep the gun in the cave. He feared that Baba might communicate with the hissing creatures and they would creep out at night and destroy it. He took it to an island in the eastern swamp and hid it in the reeds. He knew the futility of his actions. Baba simply had to read his mind to know where the gun was, but it was worth a try. He then flew the bruka to the cave and walked back home.

He reached the eastern gate wall after dark. The fire ditch threw flames twenty feet up. Beyond the flames the wall soared into the darkness, glowing in the lights from the ditch. Two men were in a tower. The watch.

"Stop!" one shouted. "Who are you?"

"It's me. Kera."

"Baba Chuma's son? What are you doing out at this time?"

"I went to fish."

He showed them a couple of tilapia he had found on his hooks. The government had started a fish farming project several years back. When war broke out, the market for the fish died, so tilapia spawned wanton in the swamps and streams. It was an easy alibi.

The watchman pressed a button, turning down the flames in the road section of the fire-ditch. They lowered a drawbridge. By the time Kera reached the gate, he felt singed.

"Only two fish?" one man said.

"There is only two of us at home," Kera said.

"Tomorrow, bring more so I can eat, too."

"No worry," Kera said. "Baba is waiting for me."

"Refugees came," the other man said. "They appeared this evening. Maybe the teacher was right all along. You see they talk of spirits fighting soldiers and telling them to come to our town."

"Oh," Kera said. He had not thought about the teacher.

"Go see them if you want," the man continued, "they are at the police station."

As he hurried to the station, Kera thought he was in a strange town. Even before the war, perpetual darkness had engulfed the town, for it did not have streetlights. When war broke out, electricity supply became erratic, so much so that it would be a miracle for the lights to come on. Now Baba must have created a generator. Hundreds of bulbs turned the night orange. His machines had repaired the buildings, giving them fresh paint and leaving no signs of the attack. A new police station, three stories high, stood in place of the old colonial structure that had been bombed out during the attack. Kera gaped. The building had gone up in just one day. He could stomach a flying machine and a flash gun, for these he had seen in a myriad of sci-fi movies, but a three-storied building that appeared out of the blue?

About thirty refugees sat on the lawn bathed in orange lights, eating supper. Steam rose from their bowls, filling the night with the aroma of goat stew and millet bread. Some had bandages. Kera recognised a few faces. When he saw the four women, a smile nearly broke out. The one whose dress the soldier had ripped off now wore a green gomesi with yellow flowers and spoon fed her baby.

About a hundred of the townsfolk had gathered. Some sat in the middle of the road. Others sat on the pavement while others stood. Many of them wore clothing made out of bark cloth. The teacher stood on the steps of the police station dressed in a bark cloth robe and shoes cut out of wood.

"I've been telling you that our ancestors are behind these miracles, and you've not listened to me," he was saying. "Now listen to these people. Hear them. I tell you it's the god Kibuuka. He has returned to save us from the puppets of the mzungu. Ma—" he started to say "Martin," but caught himself, cleared his throat, and said, "I'll never mention those kizungu names again. Asimwe, tell us what you saw."

A young man stood up. His hand bandaged, his lips torn, one eye swollen shut. He spoke with a lisp, for several teeth were broken. Though not Luo, he had lived in the town for so long that he knew the language, though he spoke with a heavy accent.

"It came from the sky," he said. "I saw the cage burning from the top downwards, which means that the source of heat was up there. The spirit shot the soldiers in the head.

Many had holes right on the top of their heads, here." He touched his pate. "I tell you, the spirit was in the sky."

Asimwe sat down.

The teacher grinned. "Kibuuka, the god of war. He can fly. He can hide up there in the clouds and rain arrows upon his enemies. Those soldiers are merely puppets of the mzungu. They care for nothing but minerals. They kill us and rape us and turn our land into ashes in the name of these useless stones. Now Kibuuka has woken up. He is fighting for us. Maybe soon we'll see Luanda Magere and Aiwel Longar and Jok Olal Oteng.

"Our town is blessed. It sits right beside the home of our ancestors." He pointed toward the valley. "They live there. This is a revival. If the spirits are to grow stronger, we must worship them the right way. They get weak when we use kizungu things—like clothes and kizungu names and kizungu religion. So, from today, we must discard everything kizungu. Everything."

Each sentence deepened Kera's frown. He wanted to shout that there was no god or spirit, only people who looked like charcoal drawings and lived inside rocks, who had no supernatural powers. They needed a machine to mend a hole in their home. He wanted to tell them he was behind it all and that he had no problem with wazungu. But a lump formed in his throat. The hissing creatures might not have been supernatural, but there still might have been a spiritual force involved. What else could explain the dreams in which he journeyed to another world to train as a superhero or his mother's voice in the sky? Maybe there were ancestral spirits involved. Maybe they had possessed the teacher, or maybe it was evil spirits.

Kera walked away in confusion. The teacher's voice fell behind him, growing fainter, but never quite fading away completely, as though the teacher had become omnipresent. Just as he turned off Main Street into Kaunda Road, which would take him to Chandi, he met two old women dressed in bark cloth. Kera did not know them. He gave them the two fish.

"Thank you," one said.

"This is our ancestors at work," another said. "We used to share everything freely until mjungu brought money. It spoilt our world."

"Take off those mjungu clothes," the first one said. "Ladit Okello is giving out bark cloth. He can make you a nice new shirt."

Like the rest of the town, Chandi was bathed in brilliant orange. His neighbourhood had never seen so much light. The houses had always been cramped close together, the walls dirty, the painting peeled off, but now the orange lights made the buildings glow as though it were a scene in an enchanted suburb. The lights were off at his home. Baba had placed blankets on the window, apparently to keep the tiny bungalow in perfect darkness. At the door Kera held his nose. A strong smell emanated from within. He wondered if Baba had died during the day and was already decaying.

"I'm still alive," Baba said from inside. The voice was his father's, but it stabbed Kera with a knife of ice. It no longer was gruff. It had a high-pitched tone that could only mean Baba was losing his power of speech. Soon Baba would hiss like a snake.

Kera pushed the door open. The smell of decomposition hit him like a gust of wind. Baba jumped away from the ray of orange light that fell in from the door. He hid in the shadows, but Kera had seen a glimpse of him. His skin seemed to have peeled off, revealing flesh full of boils that oozed pus. His hair had fallen off, leaving a few strands on his scalp. It looked as though the flesh had been scraped off to expose a skull as white and as rugged as a rock. He no longer wore glasses, for the strange shine had gone out of his eyes. In its place was something even scarier. It made Kera think of smoke whirling inside a bottle.

"It's not just the sun," Baba said, "all kinds of light hurt me now."

Kera took a step back, putting one foot out of the door. He tried to bear the smell out of respect, but he retched, fled from the doorway, and puked in the street. The door banged shut behind him, but the smell lingered, forcing itself up his nose as though it were a living thing.

*Destroy the gun*, Baba said.

Kera shivered. He had never gotten used to telepathy. It sparked off a throb in his head, but that was better than suffocating in the smell.

"I failed to save him," Kera said.

*I know. Now destroy the gun.*

"Did you know he would die?"

*I can't tell the future. I only know things that have already happened. But I know that if you don't destroy the gun it will create evil.*

"No," Kera said.

*You think you are a superhero. You are just a foolish child.*

"You can't foretell the future. How do you know the gun will make the world worse?"

*I know human nature.*

"We need it to stop the war. We need it to bring peace."

*No. You want glory. You think they'll whisper your name in the stories for thousands of years the way they whisper Kibuuka and Luanda Magere.*

Kera walked away from the house.

*Please destroy that gun.*

The smell grew fainter, but the puke left a repulsive taste in his mouth. He struggled to keep his eyes dry, but he felt something cold and wet slipping down his face. He felt as though his heart had been ripped out of his chest.

"Kera," Baba said.

Kera turned around in surprise to see Baba staggering down the street covered in blankets from head to toe and using a crutch. Kera wondered if his bones had turned to jelly. He got some satisfaction from that observation, for Baba would not be able to go to the swamp and get the gun unless he built a machine. To do that, he would have to use the workshop, and Kera intended to spend the night there to make sure Baba did not get the gun.

"Please, my son, listen to me."

"Tell me the truth. What are they?"

"You know the answer."

"Are they humans? Are they animals? Are they aliens? Are they spirits?"

"You ask too many questions, but you've already made up the answers. If I tell you our ancestors worshipped them, you'll say they are indeed supernatural. If I say they are aliens, you'll say they brought human life to Earth. If I say they are mortal creatures like you and me, you'll call me a liar and say that I refused to tell you the whole truth. So please don't ask me any more questions. I just beg you, give me the gun. Let me destroy it."

Kera shook his head and ran to the workshop.

## :: Chapter 6 ::

The workshop was empty. Machines and dead cars sat silent in the yard, gleaming in the orange lights that washed in from the streets. The teacher's voice seemed to float in with the orange rays. Chanting broke out occasionally. Kera kept hearing the word "nywol"—"birth"—over and over again. He picked up an overcoat, crawled into the van, his favourite dead car, and waited for his father.

He fell asleep, waiting. He dreamed of the ancient heroes again, but in this dream he was an invincible anti-hero. He had committed heinous crimes to keep a mzungu warlord in power. His weakness was in his eyes, and Kibuuka shot an arrow made of killer light right into his pupils.

Kera woke up with a yelp. The sun blazed right into his eyes. Screams came from far off. He threw away the overcoat and scrambled out of the car. Sweat drenched him. His shirt stuck to his skin. He wanted a bath, a dip in the cool waters of the swamp. Had Baba come in the night while he was asleep? Had he destroyed the gun? The door was latched and padlocked, but that did not mean it had stayed so the whole night.

The screaming ... It came from the street. Had soldiers attacked again?

He hurried out into the backstreet. People were pouring out of their homes. Most were dressed in bark cloth, some in crude clothing cut from goat skin. One woman wore nothing but the remains of a raffia mat around her waist. It was stiff, and he thought it cut into her flesh. She did not seem to mind. She wielded a machete.

"Sadaka!" she screamed, running.

The other people were screaming the same word. They had their backs to him. Like the woman, they all had pangas.

"Sadaka! Sadaka! Sadaka!"

*Sacrifice?*

Kera's heart stopped.

Horror headlines from before the war flashed in his head: photos of children's mutilated bodies, victims of human sacrifice, victims of some rich man's quest for wealth. With the teacher urging the town to worship ancestral spirits, someone might have thought it would please the gods if they sacrificed a child.

Kera followed the screaming maniacs round the corner onto Main Street, where a larger crowd had gathered, all half naked with bark cloth and animal skin and sisal sacks wrapped around their loins. The men's potbellies poured over the hems of their skirts while the breasts of the women sagged onto baggy stomachs. Everyone had a panga. Sunlight bounced off the blades.

"Kera!"

Kera turned. A fat man with a bush on his chest waddled toward him, rotating the machete above his head as though to imitate a helicopter's propeller. Atim's father. Atim who gave him his first taste of a woman's flesh. It seemed a million years ago. Yet hardly three months had passed. She had followed him into the valley as he took goats to graze, and she had teased him until he pulled her into a shrub. When he saw her father charging at him, he believed the fat man wanted to pulp him for what he had done.

"Kera, you mzungu lover!"

Before he could digest the phrase, someone grabbed his shirt. "Take off these slave clothes!"

An old woman grabbed his sleeve and tried to rip off the shirt. He knew her face, but he could not recall her names or how it was he knew her. Maybe she had been a good friend to his mother. Maybe she was his aunt. Maybe she had once been his teacher. All he saw was a wrinkled face with white hair and scrawny hands clawing at his shirt. "Take it off!"

Atim's father joined the old woman in tearing up his clothes. Within a few seconds a thousand fingers were on him, ripping off his shirt, ripping off his pants, ripping off his underwear. When the last piece of cloth came off, the mob threw up a loud cheer and almost immediately lost interest in him. They joined the rest of the crowd in screaming, "Sadaka! Sadaka! Sadaka!"

Kera seethed in shame, aware of his penis, small and shrivelled, cowering between his thighs. He covered it up with both hands, but no one was looking at him. Their eyes were fixed at the police station, whose walls seemed to glow in the sunlight, as they punched their machetes into the air.

Was the child they intended to sacrifice in there? Whose child was it? Had this child played with Okee and Acii?

"Sadaka! Sadaka! Sadaka!"

Kera ran fast back to the workshop. He stood just inside the gate for nearly ten minutes, listening to the screaming, allowing his heart to gradually slow down. A bitter taste stayed in his mouth, as though he had eaten a lemon rind. He wanted to spit, but his tongue was too dry. He heard the sound of marching. The chanting started to grow faint. The crowd was moving. They had probably gotten their sacrifice and were now heading out to make the offering.

*Save that child*, Kera heard a voice say. He thought it was Baba, but it could not have been Baba. Baba was far away at home, and his telepathy was effective only in a radius of a few metres.

He could not let them kill the child.

He ran about the workshop looking for something to wear. The only thing available that would look acceptable to the mob was a jute sack. His hands trembled as he ripped it apart using a shard of broken glass to make a skirt. It pricked his skin when he wore it.

The section of Main Street near the police station was empty. The crowd was about five hundred metres away, pouring out of the western gate, probably heading toward the valley. They no longer chanted "sadaka," but were singing a song that would have accompanied boys going to face the knife in a circumcision ritual.

Though he was too far to make out their movements, he knew they were stamping their feet and clapping and twisting their waists in what was supposed to be an erotic dance. Kera ran after them. He soon overtook the stragglers. They limped, for they had grown up with shoes to protect their soles and now with bare feet they staggered in pain.

Kera shoved through the mass of wriggling bodies, over the drawbridge and fire moat, and out of the town. The larger part of the crowd was already going down the slope into the valley. Vegetation obscured the front of it, but Kera grew increasingly certain that it was a child.

He could save that child. If he got his flash gun and soared into the sky, he could kill the teacher before he made the sacrifice. Then he could etch messages onto the bark of trees or on the town wall to change the course of the river the teacher had let loose.

Only when he got to the front of the procession did he see it was not a child but three adults. Father Steven and the two nuns, each stark naked and tied to a cross.

Each cross was strapped to a cart. Men pushed the carts down the slopes. The sight brought a strange kind of relief. At least they were not going to kill a child who might have been friends with Okee or Acii. Yet the horror only deepened. They were going to kill three innocent adults.

"Forgive them, Father," Father Steven was praying loudly, his voice competing with the roar of the fanatics. "They don't know what they are doing. I don't want to die like your Son, but these heathens mean to kill me like that. Forgive them, forgive them, forgive them."

The nuns were crying and trying to sing a hymn.

Kera stopped running and watched the carts go slowly down the slope. People brushed past him as they danced. Someone grabbed his hand. He pirouetted to face the mayor and the teacher. Like the previous night, the teacher wore a robe of bark cloth. This time he had a headdress as well, which made Kera think of a crown. At its front was some kind of insignia: an arrow, the sun, the moon, and stars. Was that supposed to be a representation of Kibuuka, the arrow shooter in the sky?

"There you are," the mayor said, "we were wondering about you. How is your father?"

The mayor also wore a robe of bark cloth and a headdress, though it was not as tall as the teacher's. His looked like a skullcap. It had the same insignia of an arrow in the sky. Kera felt a chill of disappointment washing through his veins. He had thought that, if he succeeded in killing the teacher, the mayor would have taken over leadership and probably would have stopped the madness.

"Glad to see you with us," the teacher said. "But jute is not African. I'll ask Okello to make you a robe. Since you are the son of Baba Chuma, our distinguished prophet, you'll get a high seat in the council."

Though they wore wooden shoes, both limped. Kera wriggled away from the mayor's grasp and bolted.

"Kera!" the mayor shouted, but the roar of the mob

swallowed up his voice, and Kera did not hear whatever else the mayor shouted.

The grass cut Kera's legs as he sped across the valley. Unlike the teacher and his men, he did not feel the pain of running barefoot. His soles were calloused. He had worn his first shoes only a couple of years ago. He soon left the mob far behind him. He could only hear whiffs of their voices.

He retrieved the bruka from the cave and flew to the swamp. He no longer cared that someone might see him. He cursed himself for keeping the gun far away. It had sounded like a good idea in the night, but with lives at stake it now felt like a mistake. He prayed that Baba had not gotten the gun. He pedaled fast. Hunger clouded his vision. He had not eaten supper. He felt his energy failing. He cursed Baba for not building an engine-powered bruka, but Baba's reasoning had been that engines pollute the environment.

*Please, Baba, don't destroy the gun.*

He prayed, he hoped, he pedalled, he huffed. The wings of the bruka made swooshing noises as they beat the air. He held his breath, knowing his world would collapse if he found Baba had taken the gun, knowing he would never have a good sleep if he failed to save the wazungu. He hoped the teacher would hold a lengthy ritual before drawing blood. That would give Kera enough time.

He reached the swamp and swooped down on the island, which was nothing more than a rock jutting out of the water. A thick growth of papyrus ensured the rock was visible and accessible only from above. Kera saw the bundle of banana fibres in which he had wrapped the gun. He landed, expecting to find the bundle empty. Baba had not taken the gun after all.

Kera jumped onto the ornithopter, invigorated, and soared, but now that he was facing the town, he saw three pillars of smoke in the distance. The miasma of failure brought out his exhaustion. His muscles ached with fatigue. He could feel the weight of his own bones. Still hoping the smoke was no indication of three burning wazungu, he climbed into the clouds and used the telephoto dial to zoom in on the fires. Father Steven and the two nuns smouldered on the crosses. Kera thought he could smell burning flesh. The mob stood in a semicircle in front of the fires, screaming, chanting, singing, though Kera could not hear a word.

It had to stop. He had failed to save the wazungu, but he could still put an end to the teacher's madness.

He aimed the gun at the teacher. His thumb trembled on the trigger button. A light press and the teacher would vanish into thin air. He could not do it. It had been easier with the soldiers, who were strangers, easier to liken them to CGI characters in *Shooter*, but here was a face he had seen all his life.

He could not do it.

Even if he killed the teacher, he could not be sure the madness would stop. There was the mayor, who he once thought was a good man, but who now seemed to be screaming the loudest with a face distorted in rage. Being a politician, seeing he could not fight the teacher, the mayor must have made a political decision to discard everything he believed in.

Even if Kera killed both the mayor and the teacher, someone else might step in. Maybe he could float down into their midst and tell them that Kibuuka had possessed him. But would that take any power from the teacher? Would that not betray the secret of the flash gun and possibly of the hissing creatures?

A better option would be to write messages on the town's wall as he had done in the barracks. They could not argue with such writing. He burned two lines above the western gate. "I hate human sacrifice. I love wazungu." The two guards atop the gate had no idea what was happening. They chewed sugarcane as they watched smoke rising out of the valley.

:::

Kera did not return to town until after dark. Again he passed through the gates with the fishing alibi. This night there were a lot more people in the streets. Some stood in clusters talking in whispers. Others had lit small fires and were engaging in rituals. Kera noticed many still wore cotton clothing, t-shirts, jeans, coats, ties, khakis, kitenges—dress that the teacher's revolution denounced as "kizungu." It warmed his heart that not everyone had joined the madness, but how long was it before the teacher turned his fury on them? Would he burn to death those who refused to denounce Christianity or Islam?

He paused at the door, sniffing for the smell of decay. Nothing. Then he noticed there were no blankets on the windows to block the light.

"Baba?" he said.

He tried the door. It swung open. The living room was empty. He listened. Nothing.

"Baba!" he shouted as he ran from room to room, flipping on lights, but his father was gone. In his parent's bedroom there was a hole in the ground and an A4-sized book beside it.

"Baba!" he shouted into the hole

He shone a torch. It was only a few feet deep. Baba had dug a tunnel to the world inside rocks, and he had sealed it behind him.

Kera tried not to cry. *I'm a big boy*, he told himself. *I am Luanda Magere, the man of stone. I am Kibuuka, the flying god of war.*

That did not stem the tears. The sound of mourning echoed in the room like a disembodied voice. He listened, as though it were someone else crying.

Knocking on the door roused him from the letter Baba had left in the first page of the book in the large, careful font of one learning how to write. The letters were spaced out neatly, almost as if the book was printed rather than handwritten. It was in Luo, so Kera had to read each sentence twice before he could grasp the meaning of Baba's words.

"I was wrong," Baba said. "I thought only weapons stir evil, but the teacher used building machines to gain his power. Maybe you are right. Maybe in the right hands technology can help our people. In this book you'll find designs and instructions on how to create many useful things, but any technology, even something like a plough, can be used for evil. I leave everything in your hands. I hope you are wise enough to discern good from evil."

Kera had flipped through the book. He saw designs for solar-powered stoves, automatic ploughs, pots that could generate water even in droughts. He was reading the letter for the tenth time when the knocks came again.

He tried to ignore them. The knocks persisted. Whoever it was could simply push open the door, but they did not. Reluctantly, Kera staggered to the door and found the teacher, the mayor, and a dozen others, all dressed in bark cloth. Kera had exchanged his jute skirt for jeans and t-shirts. Now he regretted it.

"Hello, Kera," the teacher said. "What happened to your skirt?"

Kera did not respond. The others glared at him. He felt their fingers twitching with the urge to undress him.

"See?" the teacher turned to them. "I told you, he is a fake. If he was the true Kibuuka, he would not be wearing these clothes."

"We had you followed," the mayor said.

It must have happened as he ran to the cave to get the bruka. He should have looked over his shoulders to check that no one had followed him.

"Where is your father?" the mayor said.

"This pretender stole Baba Chuma's aircraft," the teacher went on. "Baba Chuma is the true messenger, but this one, the Christian demons took possession of him and made him write that blasphemy. Our ancestors can't love wazungu. No way!"

"Where is your father?" the mayor asked again.

Kera quickly stepped into the house and slammed

the door shut. Before he could bolt it, the teacher and the mayor pushed, overpowering him. He gave up and fled to Baba's bedroom. He had to keep the book. He could not let them get it. He wished he had his flash gun. He could have vaporised them all. He wished the bruka was nearby. He could then fly away and live in the clouds where no evil existed. He ducked into Baba's bedroom and again tried to close the door, but the mayor and the teacher were right behind him.

The teacher had a machete. He wondered why he had not noticed that before. The blade sliced through his belly. He did not feel pain, but he did feel a warm liquid soaking his t-shirt, soaking his jeans. He tried to stay on his feet. He failed. He crumbled to the floor, falling face downward. He tried to get up. He could not. He was paralysed. He thought he heard a trickling as his blood flowed into the hole Baba had dug.

Someone turned him over. He saw a lizard scrambling across cracks on the ceiling. Faces stared down at him. He tried to speak. Blood filled his mouth and blocked his nostrils, choking him. He could not cough to ease the discomfort. The mayor was flipping through Baba's book, saying something. Kera could not make sense of the words. All he heard was the steady roar of a river.

# ::: Where Rivers Go to Die :::

He reached the valley where all rivers were buried and in the moonlight saw it was a lot shallower than in the stories. His body trembled with hunger and exhaustion and pain. Still, he refused to cry. Sweat clung to his skin like slime. He swayed, feeling the weight of his body on his right foot, the sole cracked and bleeding, feeling the pain of carrying his left leg, which was twisted and hanging in the air like a twig on a dead tree. They had taken away his kobi, and it destroyed his leg. They prohibited him from using a crutch, and they banished him from the village, claiming something evil had possessed him. Something that lived in the valley.

He strained his eyes examining the shadows for signs of evil. He saw nothing. He waited to feel it in the air, but he did not know what evil felt like. He only knew about it from the stories. He was a good child.

He had not meant to kill his Ma.

He knitted his brows tight to force back tears—so tight that his head hurt. He slumped onto a stone. His teeth clattered. He hugged himself for warmth and watched shadows dance as the moon raced amidst the clouds. Then it faded away, and the sun rose like a flame—like Ma's flame—behind clouds. He still saw no signs of evil in the valley.

*I'm sorry, Ma.*

The sun warmed him up, and he finally decided what to do. He would go to his aunt. She would heal his leg and give him a new life. Her village was a day's flight on a kobi. Walking, it was more than ten days. Hopping, he might take two whole moons, and he did not know the way. He would set off in a random direction, hoping to chance upon a village where they had not heard of him and ask for a map. Maybe an abiba would give him a kobi ride. He could not stay on the plateau for it was nothing but hostile rock. The valley, however, had a carpet of soft, reddish sand. It would be a short descent, just about the height of a tall tree. The cliff had enough holes to make it easy, but he wondered if, with one good leg, he would climb down comfortably.

He had been atop a tree harvesting mangoes for other children when he had learned about Ma's death. Yet, he had climbed down as though she had called him for lunch. If he had reacted with theatrical grief, maybe they would not have thought of him as evil.

He wrapped his loin cloth, the only thing they had allowed him to leave the village with, on his foot so that the blood would not make it too slick. Then he started to descend.

He lost his grip and fell. In the three heartbeats it took to reach the ground, he prayed it was hard enough to shatter all his bones and pulp his flesh. It would be a happy ending. He would not have taken his own life. Like Ma's death, it would have been an accident.

His body slammed against the sand. For a few moments he did not feel anything. A desperate hope surged that he had died and would be reunited with Ma. She would know he had not intended to kill her, *that he had not killed her.* She would love him as she had always loved him. Then the pain came. He gritted his teeth and stiffened his muscles. He wished he had his kobi. It would have stopped the agony. It would have healed him and given him a new leg.

*Why did you not heal your body, Ma? You had your kobi. Why did you choose death?*

Rage replaced pain. He fought off tears. His vision blurred, and the rocks became a vague collection of frozen smoke. The sun kissed his skin with a warmth he had not known since he was a baby snuggled in Ma's embrace, and it worsened the ache in his heart. He struggled up and hopped off in a random direction, which happened to be away from the sunrise; his shadow danced in front of him like a demon dragging him to an unknown place. His foot thudded heavily against the sand, each step jolting his body and fanning the rage. And the pain.

*Why, Ma? Why?*

He saw an object half buried in the sand. He recognized it from the murals in the Hut of Stories. He stopped in spite of the emotions burning his body and stared at the ancient metallic chair gleaming in the sun. Whatever they said about the valley was true. Something evil lived here, something that possessed him and gave him knowledge far beyond his age.

*I'm not possessed!*

He was only a little boy, too young to have a name. Ma said children could not harbour evil. The old stories said children could not harbour evil. He was good, even though he knew things that took a lifetime to learn.

A sound erupted. He jumped in fright, screaming, for now he was not alone. He fell. The sound was a *song*. The voice sounded like that of a hen, but hens did not sing. There was something weird about this tune, something eerily familiar, like something Ma loved to sing as she winnowed millet on her kobi.

Slowly, his head turned toward the sound, and he saw a creature perched on another pre-Big Burn object, which he could not recognize, but he identified the creature at once. Every story had a character like it, and every mural had a drawing of it. "Bird," the ancient people had called it. Ma said it was the ancestor of hens and that it could fly and harboured spirits of good people after they died. Then what his people called "The Big Burn" happened. It had wiped out all the birds. Since then, the spirits of good people did not have a home ... yet here was a bird in the valley of dead rivers, looking like a chick with white and black feathers, cooing a song his Ma had loved to sing.

*Ma.* He tried to speak. His jaws were like rocks, unable

to move. Something swelled in his throat, choking him. Something cold and wet rolled down his cheeks. He wiped his face with the back of his palm, but that did not stop the deluge.

*Ma.* He wept. For her. For his kobi.

She had woven the kobi the day she had given birth to him, using ten of her dreadlocks, which she had dyed a myriad of colours to create intricate designs and geometric shapes. The kobi had become his twin. It had grown with him. He slept in it at night. He went everywhere with it during the day. When older, he would have flown on it and used it as a shield. It looked like a winnower, and he used it to help Ma sieve grains of millet. Then Ma died, and they took it away, his twin, the only living part of her left, and that destroyed his leg.

*Ma*, he cried.

The bird now sounded as though it were trying to comfort him. Its beak parted to reveal a tongue made of flame—Ma's fire!

*I'm sorry, Ma.*

The bird jumped onto the sand and walked to him, singing, stepping so lightly that it did not leave footprints. Ma, now an ancestor, could not leave footprints. Yet, the bird cast a shadow. Ancestors did not cast shadows. It came close enough for him to see its eyes. They shone with a vivid blue—just like a spirit.

*I'm sorry, Ma. I didn't mean to kill you.*

The bird fell quiet. Its head drooped in sadness, and the ensuing silence amplified the solitude of the valley. He became aware of another sound that came from the bird. At first he thought it was a cat's purr, a high-pitched whirr mixed with a sonorous *clunk-clunk-clunk*. His mouth fell open in horror. Ma had once made it to demonstrate the sound of a machine.

He stopped crying abruptly. It was not Ma, even though it sang her song.

Now he noticed that its feathers gleamed and threw

pools of light onto the surrounding rocks. It confirmed the stories about the valley, that in it lived things that were as old as rocks, metals that were alive, like this bird. "Jochuma," the ancient people had called them.

He scrambled to his foot and struggled to flee. Then this was why the elders had banished him to the valley—for jochuma to find him. He would not let them. He did not belong to them. He was abiba. He inherited his gift from Ma, who got it from Grandma, who got it from her grandpa. Abiba were born as the Big Burn ravaged the world, after people cried out to ancestors for help and a fire spirit impregnated a woman whose offspring brought rain in times of drought and brought the sun when the rains caused floods. They turned barren rock into fertile farmland. They gave people tools and fuel to cook with while respecting the mother of all life, Ensi, so that over time the land would bloom again. They healed the sick. They blessed people with good luck. They did good.

They did not attempt to raise the dead.

He would have brought Ma back to life if they had let him. He knew how, though he was not old enough to make fire in his belly. Just as instinctively as he had known how to climb a tree, he had known how to put back the pieces of her body and revive her spirit. How could that be evil? He did it because his mistake had killed her. A mistake. An accident. Not evil. Not like machines. He had only wanted his Ma back.

He pushed his body hard, ignoring the pain, but he thought his foot thumped the sand like thunder and the rocks shook with each step. He tripped and fell. His chest slammed hard against a rock, and his ribs broke. Pain made his blood boil. He vomited a greenish glob of blood. He tried to get up. Pain pinned him to the sand.

He heard a hum and turned to see a flying machine with four propellers, a rusty machine slightly larger than a bull. The murals and stories depicted it as the worst. The ancient people had many names for it: "life chopper," "demon bird," "death drone," "air ogre," "destroyer." His people called it "hellbird." It transported the evil to the underworld where they paid for their sins with an eternity of agony.

*Please, no. I'm a good child.*

Its hum pricked his eardrums like a thousand spears. It landed a few paces away from him, throwing up a cloud of sand. The propellers shut down, and it fell silent. A door opened, and a short creature stepped out. It could have been human, slightly taller than a child who was old enough to get a name and marry. It had a long tail, ears that looked like bowls, and large, perfectly round black eyes with vivid blue pupils. It walked with stiff joints. Greyish steel wool covered its body to imitate fur. "Monkey," the ancient people had called it.

His stomach flared. He felt cramps, an ache—so different from the pain of broken ribs. A reassuring pain. His ancestors, after all, had not abandoned him. He was going to have his first fire. The village would have thrown him a feast and fussed over his initiation rituals to celebrate, but he was going to experience it alone in the middle of a desert with evil creatures watching. Maybe it would be big enough to melt the jochuma. When it came it was nothing more than a fart, barely singeing the sand.

It gave him hope. Fart fire was a manifestation of abiba power. In spite of all that had happened, though they had taken away his kobi, he had experienced his first fire, and he saw it as a message from the ancestors.

*Fight.*

He spread out his fingernails to suck in the sun's light. He closed his eyes, stretched his hands toward the sky. He felt a tingle in his fingernails as they connected with the clouds. He wove clouds together as though he were knitting a basket, nudging them to produce lightning and strike the jochuma. Ma had said that jochuma blood had the same energy as lightning and the only way to destroy them was to hit them with a bolt. It would be just like a person having so much blood that he drowned in it. Sparks danced on his skin, and he snapped his fingers.

Nothing.

Lightning did not strike the machine people. Without his kobi he was powerless.

The bird now hovered beside the monkey, its wings beating out a *brrrr* sound. Both looked up at the sky, where storm clouds had gathered, waiting for their death.

He snapped his fingers again and again. Still, he could not summon a bolt. His hands slumped into the sand in resignation.

The jochuma stared at the sky for a few more heartbeats and when nothing happened, turned back to him. He was too weak to cry anymore, too weak to resist when the monkey took him in its arms—cold arms, as cold as hailstone. He squirmed at the touch of metal, and the world plunged into darkness.

When he regained consciousness he was inside the hellbird. Cliffs sped past, and he knew they were still in the world of the living. He lay on a papyrus mat at the feet of the monkey, which sat on a black chair and seemed to be focused on something out of the window. The bird perched on its shoulder, looking at him. The hellbird swept into a cave. The sudden darkness made him think he had lost consciousness again. They sped down a tunnel into the underworld.

The cramps came again, the gentle ache. When the fart came, the fire was much bigger, though still not enough to melt the jochuma. It merely burned the papyrus. Darkness swallowed him up again.

When he opened his eyes, he was no longer in the hellbird. He lay in the hood of a kobi, which was woven from palm fronds and was as colourful as his had been. He had seen this type in his aunt's village. Children had snuggled in the hood, hiding from the sun, as their parents worked the gardens. This, however, was no ordinary winnower. It flew just like his kobi and Ma's kobi, though not with ancestral power. It vibrated against his body, making him nauseous, and he knew it had the jochuma life force. He was too weak to attempt jumping off.

A greenish liquid that smelled and felt like his blood covered his skin. He thought they had given him medicine to heal his wounds. He had regained some energy, and he examined his body to find the ribs were mending themselves. He checked his left leg and was disappointed to see it still twisted. It did not make sense. Was he not supposed to spend the rest of his life in agony? Why then had they given him medicine?

*Why, Ma, did you not heal yourself?*

The bird sat just outside the hood, watching him with a sad glow in its eyes while the monkey sat on the edge of the winnower, again looking off into the distance. They flew in a labyrinth of brightly lit caves, so bright that there were no shadows, no dark places, which confused him the more for he thought the underworld was a place of total darkness.

They passed by many machines. Some were gathered together as though in meetings, others looking idle, others engaged in chores. He identified many from the stories Ma had told him. He saw one fixed on a wall. They called it "chaa." It was the nightmare of every living thing. It had a wheel shape and a glassy face with twelve strange drawings and three different-coloured sticks that made a *tick-tock-tick-tock* sound. *It records time*, Ma had said. He had never understood how a machine could record time. *It is pure evil*, Ma had said. *The world descended into darkness the day it was invented. It stole away their humanity, and it dictated to them when to wake up, when to eat, when to sleep, when to have children, when to get married, and when to die. They became its slaves.*

And such a thing was inside him. No!

He loved Ma. She had invented a new tread-plough, which was a kind of machine. However, unlike jochuma, it did not have a life of its own. It required a person's input and energy to work. Ma had toiled on it for many hours to prepare the ground for planting, moving from garden to garden because ordinary folk were not allowed to use such tools. He never understood why she did not use her gifts to make the ground till itself. He hated to see her work so hard because then she had little time for him. He feared that when he grew older he would also work like that. Like a slave. He had an idea to improve the tread-plough so that she could very quickly till large swathes of land without breaking sweat, and one afternoon he fixed new parts to the plough.

He should have told her about it.

*It was an accident. Please, Ma, believe me.*

The elders told him that in improving the tread-plough he had taken the first step toward reviving automated machines and that alone was evil enough. He was possessed, they argued—a child too young to have a name could not know how to improve the tread-plough. Could not know how to bring the dead back to life.

The winnower flew through an arched gateway into a room quite unlike the caves they had passed, a room so vast that it seemed to have no walls, no ceiling, no floor, and to be full of rectangular structures that resembled the tall buildings of pre-Big Burn cities. Thousands upon thousands of them arranged in rows and columns as far as the eye could see—metallic, floating in the air, each with hundreds of tiny windows on their four faces. Inside the windows he saw people and he saw villages, oases flourishing in wastelands, round huts with drawings of flowers and long-dead animals on the walls and images of fantastical beasts on the roofs. Trees swaying above the rooftops, arid mountains looming on the horizons, white clouds in a deep blue sky providing a backdrop. People in colourful robes, some made of bark, others from softened cowskin, others woven from grass, working, laughing, drinking, making merry, fighting, playing, sitting idle under trees, singing.

Life.

Each window had the picture of an eye in one corner. Nearly all of these were a glowing green, but a few here and there, like those of the bird and the monkey, were blue. Windows, eyes: the symbols clashed in his head, and he struggled to understand their meaning.

The winnower stopped at a window. He at once recognized the village from the hut he had grown up in—a dome shape, unlike other houses, with geometric patterns instead of plants and animals decorating the walls and roof. Children laughed as they ran into view from behind the house, chasing a red ball. He was among the children, nascent dreadlocks bouncing on his head. He picked up the ball and ran to the person whose eyes were the window.

*Ma.*

Was this Ma's memory?

He had just invented a bouncing ball. He had filled a bag with air to make a tight balloon and then wrapped banana fibre around it, and the ball bounced. No one had ever played with such a ball before. Mama held it in her hand, and he remembered the frown on her face. There were two adults with her, one an elder, and both frowned at the ball.

Ma's memories.

A dry and bitter taste came to his mouth as the significance of the window dawned on him. Jochuma captured spirits of the dead who had no home since birds were extinct and imprisoned them in this underworld redolent of the pre-Big Burn cities that had created jochuma.

The next window caught his attention. The image in Ma's window played on it as well, only this was through his eyes. The ball now rolled on the ground toward Ma, who, with the two other women, pounded millet grain in a giant mortar, using pestles that were taller and heavier than their bodies. They always sang as they worked, but now they watched him with creased brows. The ball hit the mortar. Ma yelled at him to go play in the field. He could not hear, just as he could not hear the other windows. Her voice was in his own memory.

Why was his memory on this window? He was still alive … Was he?

The bird flew onto Ma's window sill and tapped on a

brick, and a ledge protruded. The monkey carried him off the winnower and lay him on the ledge. He had enough energy to sit up, though his body was stiff with fear. The monkey jumped back on the winnower and flew away, vanishing behind a row of windows, taking its whirr away, plunging the cave of memories into a deep silence. The picture on Ma's window changed to one of him sitting on her kobi as they flew above treetops on a moonlit night, going to visit his aunt. Ma had just invented an ice-making pot, and she wanted her sister to be the first to use it.

*Am I dead?*

No. He felt pain, not as severe as when he had been in the valley, for the medicine was working fast on him, but he could still feel the aches. Dead people did not feel pain.

The bird fixed him with a strange stare, as though it pitied him. The eye on Ma's window was green while that on his was blue—just like the bird's. He had brown eyes. Ma had had brown eyes, too. What did the blue and green stand for? The living and the dead? The bird touched Ma's window-eye with the tip of a feather, and it turned red. "Maatin'na," Ma said, her soft voice disturbing the silence of the cave.

His blood turned into hailstone. His flesh turned into lava. *Ma's voice.* It sounded different, as though she were speaking from inside a pot, but it was Ma's voice coming out of the bird: *My first and only son* ... which was what she had always called him. When he was younger he used to think that was his name. "I love you," Ma said, the bird's beak moving eerily to spew out the words. His eyes clouded with tears. "I never stopped loving you."

He did not know whether to still be angry with her, to rejoice that he had found her spirit or to worry that he was in the underworld without being dead. "I hate to see you in such grief," Ma said. "Don't blame yourself. It was an accident. The plough chopped me to pieces, and I couldn't touch the kobi to rebuild my body."

His confusion deepened. How could it be her memory

yet she was talking to him in the present? The confusion made his head ache. His vision blurred. He closed his eyes as tears slipped out, and he heard a cry as if it came from another person. "Don't cry, maatin'na. I never died. I lost my body, but I didn't die."

Her words tumbled in his skull like an avalanche of rocks. He closed his eyes tighter and prayed this was all a dream. A nightmare. *I didn't die.* It could only mean that she had no spirit. That he had no spirit. That the story about their origin was not true. That someone must have concocted the fable of the fire-spirit to make abiba more acceptable to humans who, because of the Big Burn, abhorred machines and the quest for knowledge that machines represented. The evidence was in the window with his memories, though he was not dead. Somehow jochuma had access to his consciousness. Yet no one, not even spirits, could access another human's brain. It could only mean that he was not human. Maybe he was a species of jochuma. "I still love you. I never stopped loving you. You are a rare gift to—"

He willed his ears to shut, and it cut off Ma's voice.

*No. Not Ma. It could not be Ma.*

Jochuma were playing a trick on him. They had stolen Ma's spirit and imprisoned it in a metal box and were using it to deceive him.

He was not a jochuma.

He was abiba. He was conceived in a womb. He had a father, who died when he was a baby. He had a grandmother on whose laps he loved to play. Jochuma could not be born. They were made. Manufactured. He was abiba, a muchwezi, a demigod. He had a spirit. He was good.

Eyes still closed, he pushed himself off the ledge and fell. Cramps flared in his belly. He farted a huge cloud of fire. Windows sped past him as he plummeted. Thousands of captured memories flashed by. His scream echoed off the metal. The windows caught the light from his fire, and he thought he was burning it all down. He fell for a long time. He began to panic, thinking he would not hit a floor. He would fall forever with other people's memories pulsing around him. For a moment he regretted having thrown himself off the ledge.

Then he saw the winnower directly below him a moment before he crashed into it, rocking it, almost upsetting it. His fire went out with a *pssh*, the same sound his ball made while deflating. He ignored the pain that surged through his body and scrambled to escape; but the bird touched his temple with its wing, and darkness swallowed him.

When he opened his eyes, he was under a tree. A dying tree with only a few withered leaves clinging to the branches. He felt his kobi before he knew that he lay on it. He sat up abruptly and looked at it in disbelief. His kobi, woven with Ma's dreadlocks, colourful with intricate designs and geometric shapes, throbbing with life, happy to reunite with him. His leg had grown back, too, and he did not feel any of the injuries he had sustained in the valley.

What had happened? Had it all been a bad dream? Was Ma still alive?

He noticed a black-and-white feather stuck on his kobi. He touched it and discovered it was, unlike a chicken's feather, made of metal. Bits of grey steel wool clung to one end.

It had happened. Ma was dead, her spirit trapped in a metallic box.

About twenty people had gathered under a nearby tree, which was also dying. They sat on three-legged stools in a circle, talking to themselves in low tones. They were all elderly. A village loomed in the distance, the houses looking gaunt, hazy behind the mirages. Unlike those in his village, which were round, these were rectangular. Tufts of yellowish grass struggled to stand upright in the scorched land. Mountains he could not recognize loomed on the horizon, red and bare. Not a cloud stood in the sky, which was the colour of ash.

"He stood up," one woman said, loud enough for him

to hear. She was looking at him. He frowned. He was not standing up. Were they talking about someone else? Then it came to him that she had spoken in a strange dialect. What she meant was "he woke up." He noticed that their clothes, their hairstyles, the jewellery on their shriveled skins belonged to a people he had never heard of before. He was very, very far away from the world he knew.

He rose to his feet, clutching his kobi, as the old people made their way to him. Ribs showed through skin, tummies sucked in to expose hip bones. Robes hung loose on them, and their hair seemed about to fall off. They stopped at a respectful distance, as if he would bite, and fell to their knees, hands clasped in front of their chests. They bowed down to him.

"We don't have an abiba," the woman said, keeping her eyes on the dying grass at her knees. Her voice crackled with thirst. Her lips were dry and peeling. He hoped he was correctly interpreting her words. "We wronged Mother Life. We thought the ancestors would never forgive us. We hope they sent you as a sign that they have forgiven us."

He thought about what his mother had said in the cave of memories. He looked at the black-and-white feather and he thought about the bird and the monkey. A sharp pain hit his heart, and his eyes welled up. He blinked hard, determined not to cry in front of these strangers. He wondered if he would forget his mother. He wondered if he would find a new mother in this village, a new home. He promised himself not to do anything foolish again, like trying to make an automated machine or trying to raise the dead. He would not lose another home.

"I'll serve you," he said. "I'll be your god."

# ::: The Green Men Who Fly :::

*26th October 1850*

Colonel Stone arrived today. The Prince, Father John, and I went to Ngoro Bridge to meet this famous soldier and his band of forty warriors. A hundred natives, sagging under loads of military hardware, and the soldiers' personal luggage stood weary behind the white men. Two of Colonel Stone's fighters were in stretchers with malaria. They'll miss the expedition to the unexplored jungle beyond the waterfalls to attack the Ndegeges and capture their flying machine.

Col. Stone is a huge, never-smiling Gorilla with a face full of beards and long hairs all over his arms. He shook Father John's hands with such violence that the priest still complains of a shoulder ache. He almost spat into my palms when I tried to greet him. He didn't accept the Prince's hands either. Customarily, we don't greet with a shake of hands, but Father John had cautioned us to make the soldiers feel at home.

"This is Prince Thenge," Father John said, gestured toward the Prince. "The men behind him are his servants. This is Simon," he smiled and wrapped a hand around my shoulders. "My disciple. His father was the first Christian convert. I've lived with this boy since he was five years old. He can read and write. He's keeping a diary and is now a teacher to his people." I smiled at the soldiers.

"Congratulations," the colonel said. "You are a genius."

The other soldiers laughed. The colonel didn't. I wondered what was funny. I later asked the priest what the word *genius* means, and he told me it's someone who is very, very intelligent. Then I asked him why the soldiers laughed when the Colonel referred to him as a genius. He didn't reply.

"Where's the camp?" the big soldier asked as the laughter died out.

"Yes," Father John said. "We've built you and your men enough houses, and we've assigned you servants. But your men must not touch any of the young girls who'll be attending to them. We don't want to create trouble for the church."

"Boys," the colonel said to his men, without taking his eyes off the priest, "who wants to lay a monkey?"

Another bout of laughter. I didn't get this joke either. I didn't even understand his question, though I know "to lay" means to put something down, or to prepare something, for example, a table for a meal. These soldiers talk and think in a manner Father John never taught me.

"There's a big welcome party for you," Father John said. "The natives are overwhelmed by the appearance of forty white men. They'll celebrate for a week."


*27th October 1850*

Father John and Col. Stone had a meeting this morning. They sat under a shed in the flower garden behind the priest's home. I made them tea. Stone wanted wine. Father John said drinking in the morning was a sin. The soldier then talked in a very strong language, said he'd tell their Queen about the priest's inhospitality and that should the mission fail, it would be because Father John hadn't fully cooperated. He still didn't get the wine.

The priest spread a map on the table. The unexplored jungle where the Ndegeges live, about five miles up the river beyond the waterfalls, is a green smudge. It makes up half the map. The other half shows the King's Palace, the villages, the stream, and the Church, which sits on a knoll near the evil forest. The King allocated the church this site, hoping the location would deter his subjects from converting to the white man's religion. Father John believes Church Hill, as he named it, is a good military position to hold. It commands a bird's view of our land, and if one climbs up the bell tower, one can see far into the jungle, though you can't see anything beyond the waterfalls.

"One day," he said to the soldier, "I was admiring the forest from the tower with my spyglass. I saw a green man flying over the trees. I thought it was a hallucination. I made inquiries. No one told me anything. The natives believe that even mentioning the green people's name brings bad luck. Simon's father told me everything I needed to know."

Father John had wanted to go into the forest and find out about the Ndegeges and their flying machines. My father wouldn't let him. He said that those green men were cannibals and that they kept other human beings the same way we kept cattle. Father John then sent a letter to his Queen, and she sent Colonel Stone. She was determined to capture the green people's flying machine. It would make her Empire the most powerful on earth.

Father John produced a drawing he'd made of a green man in air. "This is what they look like," he said.

Colonel Stone closely examined at the picture. "Do they paint themselves green?"

"Yes."

"What kind of weapons do they have?"

"We don't know anything about them. No one has ever had contact with them. The natives fear to go into the forest. They say it's infested with evil. Only a few old men had ever seen them before I came. One flew right over their huts a long time ago."

"I want to see for myself," the Colonel stood up.

"Sure. It's noon. They always fly between now and three o'clock."

"If it's a wild goose chase, I'll shoot you in the head."

We went up the tower. We had to wait until two o'clock

before one appeared. We couldn't see much with naked eyes, just the speck of a bird in the distance. The Colonel used the spyglass until the mirage dived back into the jungle.

"What did I just see?" he whispered.

"Let's go back down now," Father John said. "They won't be coming out again until tomorrow."

"Have you ever seen more than one?"

"Yes, once, about twenty flew in circles like birds in formation. Must have been some sort of ritual."

"Where did they get that machine? They live in the middle of a jungle. They're just animals. How then did they build a flying machine?"

Father John had no answer.

*1st November 1850*

Finally, the forty soldiers set off up the river to face the Ndegeges. We watched from the bell tower as they rowed the rafts against the strong currents. It took them over two hours to get to the waterfalls and three hours more to scale the cliff and haul their gear using makeshift pulleys over the fifty foot-high cataract. We couldn't see anything beyond the waterfalls. When the last man disappeared, we started to pray.

Col. Stone's artillery opened fire an hour later. We heard several big bangs. Almost immediately, nearly thirty creatures darted out of the greenery and flew to the sky. The cannons continued to explode. Huge columns of smoke spewed over the jungle. The Ndegeges hovered above the battlefield like vultures waiting for a signal to descend upon a carcass. For thirty minutes the guns thundered, and the green men circled above the trees.

Then, all of a sudden, the artillery fell silent. In unison the flying people dived back to their mysterious world. Nothing remained in the scene apart from smoke that petered out in half an hour.

We kept watch in the tower up to late in the day. It was my turn with the telescope. I saw something falling off the cliff, something dark against the white beam of water on the cataract. It was a man. He plunged into the rivers. When he came up, I saw it was the colonel. He swam desperately. The currents helped him in his escape.

"They lost the battle," Father John said. "He's probably the only survivor."

We ran down to the river to wait for him. He seemed to take forever to reach civilized land. When he did, he was out of strength. He couldn't talk. His right arm had turned green. We at first thought the Ndegeges had painted him, but when Father John tried to wash off the dye, we discovered his skin color had changed irreversibly. The new color steadily spread to the rest of his body. By the time we retired, he was green from head to toe.

*2nd November 1850*

Colonel Stone recovered his tongue this morning. He told us there were no machines in the forest, just a wrecked metallic tube full of green creatures with wings. He didn't know that the skin on his back had split to give birth to wings, cockroach-like wings. We locked him up in the barn. We fear to let him out.

Father John has started another letter to his Queen. He calls the wrecked metallic tube a "Spacecraft" and the green men "Martians." He hasn't explained any of these terms, but he says they mean a lot of trouble.

# ::: The Terminal Move :::

Laceng walked to the end of the world. That is how the story of our people starts. I tell it to you, as I heard it from my grandfather, who was there with Laceng at the edge of a plateau, looking down into a valley at a spectacle their young eyes had never seen. Behind lay the land in which they had lived all their lives. It was flat and harsh, full of sand and rocks. The desolate aura allowed only a few kinds of plants to grow, miserable grains, tufts of reddish grass, thorny shrubs, short withered trees. The rains were sporadic, the water holes few and muddy, the streams thin and seasonal. In front, deep below at the base of the wall holding up the tableland, a mighty river flowed, calm and gentle. It made them think of a giant snake crawling away into the sunset. Flowers grew wantonly along its banks and amid the lavish green of the vale, painting the land with a myriad of colors, creating beautiful patterns that could only be the artwork of jok. They emitted a sweet smell that wafted through the golden mist, reminiscent of aroma from a lover's pot. Tinged with the hues of sunset, the foliage emblazoned the river with warm and beautiful tones. Far in the distance, bluish mountains rose into the clouds. To the left, in the shadows of the approaching dusk, a vast jungle stretched into the horizon. Gently, the sun slid into this thick forest.

"Wow," Laceng said to my grandfather, Ganzi, his closest friend. They were one of the many teams scouting for new land, and it could only be jok that had guided them to stumble upon this paradise.

"Look at how tall and big the trees are!" Ganzi said. "Look at all that water!"

"This is our new home!"

167

"Yes!"

They hugged each other and danced in celebration. But then a cloud swept over Ganzi's face, wiping off his smile. Laceng knew what he was going to say before he spoke.

"Oh, well," Ganzi said. "I hope the elders like it."

Their position gave them a bird's view of the entire valley. They could not see signs of a settlement. There was just a continuous lushness and colourful expanse.

"It is empty," Laceng said. "It's fertile. It has water. It has colour. It smells nice. Why would they refuse to settle here?"

Our people were called the Jolabong back then. They had become wanderers shortly after Laceng was born. They once had a home that was as beautiful and fertile as this valley, but a hostile tribe from the northern desert envied their lush hills and sparkling springs. The ensuing war lasted a whole moon. The invaders won. The Jolabong fled.

They wandered in the wilderness searching for a new home. They passed strange lands with strange plants. They could not tell the edible from the poisonous until too late. They encountered cannibals, savage tribes, evil peoples who made pots out of skulls, peaceful and friendly nations who nevertheless did not welcome them. Wherever they tried to settle, disaster struck. Sometimes the new country was infertile. Other times long spells of drought sent them hurrying away—but most times stronger people drove them out. Many of them died. The harsh life made their women barren. Their population dwindled. They faced extinction.

As Laceng looked into this valley with the warmth of the sun on his face, a famous proverb rang in his head. No journey lasts forever, all roads lead somewhere, each odyssey ends the way it started. Theirs had to end here.

The next day he and Ganzi joined the expedition to explore the valley because they had found it. They were the youngest in the group, unmarried, the only ones not yet initiated into adulthood. They set off from the camp at dawn and reached the plateau wall shortly after sunrise.

Pinyi, a seasoned warrior with battle scars all over his body, led the expedition. As captain of the kondo, the warrior guardians of the tribe, he wore a lion's skin over his shoulders though he had never killed or fought one before.

The team comprised of ten other warriors and Gutu the healer, a tiny old man with a wrinkled skin and a pocked face but a body that still had the potency of youth. He wore a tortoise shell and carried a staff bedecked with charms. He had a red gourd strapped to his waist. It shook whenever it encountered evil. The strength of its shaking advised the elders on whether to settle in a land. To Laceng's dismay, the gourd emitted a sharp rattling sound the moment Gutu saw the mountains.

"Something evil lives up there," the medicine man said.

Laceng looked at the wrinkled fingers curled tightly around the neck of the gourd. He wondered if the gourd really shook on its own, if spirits really lived inside it, if these spirits really trembled in the presence of evil. He looked at the pocked face sticking out of the tortoise shell, a face he once thought was full of wisdom.

"Evil?" he said. "You see evil in this beauty?"

"Shut up," Pinyi said. "You are just a child."

The heat of anger rushed into Laceng's face. He did not like being called a child. He was sure he could beat Pinyi in a fight. He was as tall as the warrior, his shoulders were as broad and his chest as big, but his good looks betrayed his tender age.

"We might never find a place—" he began, but Pinyi screamed at him.

"Shut up!" The kondo had a big voice. It thundered over the valley and brought a long moment of silence. He added, almost whispering, "One more word from your ignorant mouth and you'll go back to the camp to pick firewood for the mothers."

Laceng bit his lips to suppress the anger and swallow his pride, to stifle words that threatened to explode from his mouth. They were in a strange land, which their ancestors and gods knew nothing about. How then could Gutu discern evil at first sight? He bit his lips so hard that he tasted blood.

"Should we go down?" Pinyi asked the medicine man. "Is it safe?"

"Yes," Gutu said. "It was only a slight shake. We might still make this our new home."

"Good," Pinyi said. "It does look like the home we used to have."

They puzzled over how to go down the deep plateau wall. They spent most of the morning searching the edge until they found a path. It was not a natural cleft. Someone had hewed a zigzag road on the steep rock surface. Whoever made it had abandoned it ages ago. Weeds had grown over the steps. A sign warned against going down. Three skulls sat on poles at the mouth of the path. Birds had built nests in them, impervious to their lingering warnings.

"See?" Gutu said, his eyes on Laceng. "There can be evil in beauty."

He waited for his gourd to shake. It did not.

"Maybe someone just wanted to scare people away from their territory," Laceng said.

"Maybe," Gutu said. "But why do they not live here anymore? Why is the place empty?"

He took a hesitant step down the path. He glanced at his gourd. It stayed silent. He descended. The path made it an easy climb for him in spite of the tortoise shell. The others followed. As they went down, holding the rock surface for fear of falling off the zigzag path, Laceng wondered how the mysterious builders had created such a road. They must have been very clever people with powerful tools.

Once at the bottom, they could not cross the river. The water was deep. They could not swim. The smell of flowers was strong, filling the air with a freshness that made Laceng smile. Many types of fish swam in abundance. Butterflies floated about like happy spirits. Birds sang to welcome them. Plenty of animals came to drink, some looked easy to domesticate. The trees were even taller when viewed from down here. The bank on this side was too narrow, too full of rocks, to allow for proper exploration.

Laceng glared at Gutu's treacherous gourd, daring it to shake. It stayed silent.

They brought down banana stems to make rafts. The next day they succeeded in crossing the river, and over the following several days they explored the land. They went shortly after sunrise and hurried back up before sunset. Though he longed to spend nights in the beautiful valley, Laceng could not ignore the danger signs. They discovered that the river came down from the mountains and flowed into the thick forest. The vale was thus enclosed with the jungle, the mountain, and the endless plateau wall forming natural borders. They found ruins of a settlement. It increased their worry. It proved that another tribe had lived there, but why did they abandon such a paradise? Laceng waited for Gutu's gourd to shake with an answer. It did not until they followed the river to the doors of the jungle. The gourd gave a shrill noise, a scream of agony. It hurt Laceng's ears. His eyes welled up in pain and anger.

"No," Gutu said once the gourd went silent. "There is a terrible evil in this forest."

Tears rolled down Laceng's face. He did not want them to know he was crying. He fell to his knees and buried his head underwater. It was cool, a solace from the scorch of noon. He stayed submerged for a long time, until he ran out of air. When he came up for breath, a comforting hand touched his shoulder.

"Son," Gutu said. "Trust our ancestors. They will lead us to a new home soon."

Laceng shook the old man's hand off. He stood up. He thought about the skulls, about the abandoned settlement. He looked at the forest. What could be in there? He looked at the flowers and the fruits in the trees. He heard the birds, the breeze, the river whispering, a small voice telling him that this was home. He turned to Gutu.

"How do you know they did not lead us here?" he said.

"Hey!" Ganzi shouted. It was unthinkable to question the wisdom of Gutu.

Pinyi rushed forward and slapped Laceng, the way he hit his children to discipline them. Laceng parried the blow and punched the warrior in the face. Pinyi fell into the water. When he scrambled out, his nose was bleeding. He charged at Laceng, but Gutu shoved his staff between them. Pinyi stopped, panting in rage.

"No need to fight," Gutu said. "The child asks a wise question. I can't answer him. When he grows older he will find the answer."

The insult doubled Laceng's anger. His pride swelled. He looked into Gutu's eyes and started his rebellion.

"I will go into the forest," he said.

"You won't come out alive," Gutu said.

"And if I do?" Laceng said. "Shall we make this our home?"

Gutu shook his head. "I've never heard the gourd scream like that," he said. "There is a terrible evil in there. It will kill you. Don't go."

Laceng jeered, walked past Gutu, and headed for the jungle, which lurked in the distance. Ganzi jumped upon him and wrestled him to the ground.

"Don't go!" Ganzi cried.

They fought, but Laceng was stronger. He shoved Ganzi into the water. The kondo jumped on Laceng and threw him back into the mud. Laceng fought them, but he could not beat all ten men. They pinned him in the mud.

"We won't allow your foolishness to let you commit suicide," one of them said.

"Let him go," Gutu said.

Laceng scrambled to his feet. He wiped the mud off his body as he hurried away.

"On the day you were born," Gutu said, "I prophesied that you would be a great leader of our nation." Laceng stopped, listening, but did not turn around to face the old man. "I stand by my words. You will be our great leader, but your time has not yet come. Please listen to the wisdom of the ancestors. Let them groom you to fulfill your destiny."

For a long moment Laceng stood still, the words sinking into his head. The three skulls floated in his vision, the abandoned settlement simmered like a mirage. He closed his eyes tight and thought about how nice it would be to live amidst the scent of the flowers.

He marched to the jungle.

Blood rushed through his veins like rapids in a shallow river. As he got closer to the forest, he noticed the absence of flowers, almost as if they were afraid of the woods. Instead of their perfume, a stench filled the air. The smell grew stronger with each step he took. It was so strong at the mouth of the jungle. He stopped for a moment, aware he was too far from the expedition for them to hear any scream for help. He armed his bow with an arrow and hesitantly marched into the darkness, which was so thick that it formed a solid mass of terror beneath the trees. An eerie silence screamed at him. The river did not hum. The frogs did not croak. He did not hear insects or birds. There was just a deep silence, an empty darkness, as if he had gone blind and deaf.

When he did hear a rustling, he thought he had imagined it, until he saw a pair of green eyes and a set of white teeth. He did not stop to think. He shot the arrow and struck the creature. The eyes and teeth vanished. A thud boomed as the thing crashed to the forest floor. He did not wait to see more eyes and teeth. He spun around and fled. His knees felt like rotten bananas.

Once he was safe in the sunlight, he stopped. He turned back to look into the darkness of the jungle. He thought he saw thousands upon thousands of eyes and teeth in the darkness. He thought he heard a low hoot, a sonorous sound like the howl of a dog.

:::

That night the Circle of Elders met. It comprised of fifty old people. They sat on tiny three-legged stools in a circle around a fire, which negated the chill that the moon cast down. Each elder had a long straw to suck alcohol from clay pots. Laceng wanted to attend the meeting, to discredit Gutu's argument that they should move because of a great evil in the forest, but he could not. He was too young to even share a pot with any of the old people. So he summoned the unmarried youth around a much bigger fire and fanned the flames of rebellion.

"Are you not tired of walking?" he asked them. "Don't you want to build your own huts in a land you call home? Gutu says we cannot stay here because there is evil in the forest. But I saw this evil. It had green eyes and white teeth. I killed it. We cannot keep running away because an old man shakes his gourd and wants us to think the ancestors are speaking to him. We have to make this our home."

"What happened to the previous inhabitants?" someone asked. "Why is such a beautiful, fertile land full of game and sweet smelling flowers empty of people?"

Many youths refused to listen to him. They walked away. Laceng thought they would all desert him until a hand warmer than the fire touched his shoulder. Deyu, whose pretty face had a smile that shone with the happiness of the crescent, whose thick lips gave her face two colors, for they looked like the bottom of a pot while the rest of her skin had the rich sepia of wood.

"I'll stay with you," she said, her voice as soft as the breeze. "I love the flowers."

They had fallen in love when the yellow people attacked three moons ago. They had been hiding behind a huge rock. The moon lit up her face, and he could see his image in her eyes as clearly as though he were looking into a mirror of clear water in a pond. The next morning he gained the courage to organize a defense, which saved the tribe from annihilation. Some say she advised him on how to defeat the yellow people, some say without her, he would not have evolved into the leader we celebrate today in our songs and stories. My grandfather said that since that night behind the rock, every time she touched Laceng, he felt the power of lightning in her fingers. A calmness settled upon his heart, and peace engulfed his soul.

"My fellow lutino," she said to the rest of the youth, raising her voice such that even those who were walking away could hear. "Before you all leave, please remember Gutu's powers. Was he lying when he prophesied about Laceng on the day that he was born?"

Many stopped to listen. A few returned.

Laceng was born during a ceng-ki-dwe, a solar eclipse. In the middle of the day, his mother started to scream in birthing pains just as total darkness came down. She gave birth and died in the process. The boy's first cry brought light back to the world. They named him Laceng. Son of the Sun. Gutu prophesied that he would one day lead the nation out of dark times.

"You speak well, Deyu," Ganzi said. "Maybe our ancestors are finding it hard to keep up with us since we are constantly moving. Maybe this has affected Gutu's powers. I was there. I heard him say that Laceng will not come out of the forest alive. But look, isn't this Laceng?"

"Gutu also said that Laceng's time has not yet come. But look, many of us still have wounds from fighting the yellow people. Our kondo were defeated. Our nation faced annihilation. But Laceng saved us. Even before getting married or passing through the kwarkondo ritual, he became a warrior and led us to victory. What more proof does anyone need? I say his time has come!"

A few youths cheered. Ganzi went down on his knees in front of Laceng, bowed, and beat his chest three times. Deyu followed suit. One by one, the young people knelt in front of Laceng and pledged their allegiance to him. Those who refused to rebel walked away. His followers stood in a circle around him, expectation glowing on their faces. He felt the weight of the task on his shoulders. The enormity of what he had done sunk in. He had created a division in the nation.

"Thank you," he said. "Now I have to speak to the elders."

He touched Deyu's shoulders and looked into her eyes for inspiration and courage before walking to the Circle of Elders. Custom had it that no one must interrupt the meeting, especially not someone barely out of his childhood. Laceng stopped a respectful distance from the old people. They fell silent on seeing him, reproach blazed on their wrinkled faces. He went down on his knees and bowed his head.

"My parents," he said, "I do not wish to break up the nation. Gutu is a wise man. If he says we shall find a home soon, I believe him. But we are tired of walking. We might walk until our hair grows as white and wise as yours before we find a home. You, the old ones, should be the tired ones, but no, it's us, the children, who have decided to make this our home."

A long silence followed. He dared not look up at them or he would lose his courage. He knew they were all looking at him, scrutinizing him with failing eyesight. When someone spoke, it took him several moments to recognize Gutu's voice. It trembled with such rage that it lost its soft, fatherly qualities.

"Your time has not yet come!"

"I know," Laceng said. "I beg you to forgive me. But I insist, the great evil in the forest can be defeated. Give us time to fight it. Let us stay for a few moons. If we fail, we will have no choice but to keep walking. That is all we are asking for—time."

He rose to his feet, bowed again, and walked away from them.

The Circle of Elders continued to deliberate long into the night. The next morning they announced their decision. The entire nation gathered to listen.

"This land is beautiful and fertile," Gwotu, the caretaker king, said. "But we cannot stay. There is a great evil in the forest. However, our food supplies are diminishing. We must plant soon, or else we shall starve. We will stay for only six moons. After the harvest we shall resume searching for a new home."

Laceng smiled. He had gotten the time he asked for, though he thought six moons were not enough. It would be better to watch the land over a complete circle of seasons, thirteen moons.

That same day, as some people went down to identify places where they could easily set up their farms, Laceng and his followers plotted to build a town. They picked a spot along the riverbanks as far away as possible from both the forest and the mountains, the two potential sources of evil. The plateau wall meant they could not settle any more than half a morning's walk from either place.

"We need to think in terms of defense," Laceng said. "First, we must build a wall around our town, a high wall with positions at the top for us to shoot an invading enemy."

"And we need weapons," Deyu said. She knew a lot about plants and herbs from her grandmother, and everyone there knew that when she said weapons, she did not mean bows and arrows. She had ideas about mass poisons, fiery explosives, and things that were still vague concepts in her head. "We need weapons."

The land was full of very tall trees with wide trunks. They cut these down and planed them, using a combination of fire and stone axes. The tall trunks enabled them to make a wall twice as high as a hut. An old man called Logeto, who had the gift of building things, designed watchtowers at the top of the fence, from where archers could shoot arrows. They went into the valley just after sunrise and ran back up before darkness fell. They feared to spend nights in the valley before the wall was complete.

For ten days they worked without trouble.

On the eleventh day evil descended from the mountains in the form of giants.

Laceng and his followers did not hear about it until it

was nearly too late. They were working in their town far from the rest when someone ran to them with the news that monsters had attacked. At first, Laceng thought of the tall creatures in folklore, and he wondered if Deyu had already come up with a weapon to defeat such an enemy. He held his bow ready and raced to the spot where they were said to have gathered. Pinyi and Gutu were already there, talking to the behemoths. There were about six giants. He was relieved to see that they were only slightly taller than a normal man. They looked obese, not with fat but with muscle and bones. Each weighed the same as three men put together. They carried knives made out of a strange material. Laceng could see his image in each blade. The knives were as long as his arm and glinted in the sunlight. They wore animal skin instead of bark and had fearsome war paint on their faces. One had leopard skin draped over his shoulders. His hair was styled to imitate goat horns. He did all the talking.

Gutu knew many tongues. He could understand some of their words, but they relied on signs and drawings to communicate. From the images Laceng saw on the ground, the giants were asking them to leave. They talked with Gutu for a long time. When they were sure they understood each other, they left.

"They are the Kalaba," Gutu said. "Distant cousins of the Keroba, who used to live near us long before most of us were born. They sinned. Their gods destroyed them with fire and stones from a mountain. The remnants wandered about until they reached here and made a home in the mountains. We have unknowingly followed their footsteps."

"So they would let us settle here," Laceng said. "If we were their neighbors long ago, they will not drive us away, will they?"

"They want us to leave immediately," Gutu said. "Or else their army will come after tomorrow to drive us out."

"But why? They do not use the land. Why can't they let us stay?"

Gutu ignored Laceng. He walked away. The young people followed him, pecking him with questions. He kept his mouth shut until he climbed back up the plateau to the camp. The whole nation was already gathered, waiting to hear about the giants. Gutu asked the Circle of Elders to meet, though it was not yet evening. The old people assembled in a tent. Laceng could not wait to hear everything later. No one ever knew how long these meetings lasted. He went against custom and sat near enough to the tent to overhear what Gutu told the elders.

It drove fear into him. For the rest of the day, one word whistled in his head like a shrill horn. Finally, he had a name for the green eyes and white teeth. Jothokwo. The dead are living, not in the benign manner of long gone ancestors who protect them, but in the terrifying fashion of a corpse with a spirit trapped inside it. Dead, rotting, but alive.

"And hungry," Gutu said. "They are cannibals. They eat nothing but living people, or else they starve to a second death when the spirit leaves the body and proceeds to the world of the dead. It takes about fifteen circles of seasons for a dead body to starve to a second death. That is what the Kalaba are hoping for. That is why they live up in the mountains and not in the valley. It's now been ten circles of seasons. In another five the jothokwo will die out. The Kalaba are afraid that if we stay here for much longer, we shall provide them with a new life. The Kalaba cannot let that happen. We must leave tomorrow or fight them."

A long silence followed. Though outside, Laceng could feel the mood in the hut. They would rather move than waste lives in fighting giants. After the war with the yellow people, which left half of their kondo dead and the remaining half wounded in spirit, they could not engage in another war. Not against giants.

"Why have these jothokwo not yet attacked us?" one elder said.

"Good question," Gutu said. "It's a good thing everyone followed my advice and no one stayed down there after darkness. The jothokwo can't walk in sunlight. They come out of the forest in the night."

"Well, then," Gwotu the caretaker king said, "we could stay up here and only go down during the day to get water from the river and grow crops."

"The Kalaba want us to leave immediately," Gutu said. "They cannot risk losing what they have gained so far. Their army will come in two days. We cannot defend ourselves. We simply cannot. We must march with the first light."

Laceng was afraid. The green eyes and white teeth haunted him, but he had killed one with an arrow. Did that not mean that the fearsome living corpse was vulnerable?

He walked away from the tent. The entire nation stood at a respectful distance, waiting until the meeting ended to know what had been discussed. The older folk eyed Laceng with contempt. In their eyes he saw what they thought of him, a rebel against culture, a rash young man doomed to a fatal end, an impatient fool unable to wait for the right time to fulfill his destiny. His followers were proud that he had done it. They crowded around him, a million questions in their eyes.

"Let's prepare to defend our land," he said.

He kept walking, did not wait to see who had heard him or who would still follow him. A hand touched his shoulders, lightning struck. He smiled in happiness. Deyu was coming with him. Her mother was screaming at her. Laceng felt lucky that he did not have any elderly blood relative to contend with. His father died shortly after he was born. His grandmother raised him, but she too passed away when he was still a little child. He had lived with many caretaker families like many of his orphaned peers, but he did not owe any allegiance to anyone. He felt free to rebel.

Deyu's mother was screaming something to this effect, something about parentless degenerates ripping children from their mothers. Laceng ignored her. So did Deyu. So did other youth who followed him. They were miserably few. Most were afraid to leave the protective comfort of their elders. Would he have enough fighters to defend the land against the giants and the jothokwo?

He swam across the river. Many of them had learnt how to swim in that short period of time. They were not yet comfortable in the water, but they could float and propel themselves to the other side. The glee with which his followers jumped in reminded him that these young people were only thinking of fun. They did not want to go on another trek through desolate lands, going hungry and thirsty for days. The way they laughed as they splashed water indicated that they were not thinking of the giants.

On the lush bank Laceng sat on a stone with Deyu, holding hands, their feet in the water. He watched his followers flocking to him. Those not courageous enough to swim came in rafts. Scores more were coming down the cleft on the wall like a column of ants. The adults appeared on the plateau wall. They were too far away for him to see their faces, but he could feel the anger. A woman stood at the edge of the plateau as though she wanted to throw herself to death. The blue paint on her bark robe blended with the sky. Deyu's mother. She was wailing for her daughter to come back up.

"It will be all right," Laceng said to Deyu, wiping the tears that rolled silently down her cheeks. "Come on. Don't cry. It will be all right."

Ganzi swam fast to their feet. He was breathless when he broke out of the water.

"I know how we can defeat the giants!" he said. Laceng frowned at him. "They didn't have arrows. They had long knives. I don't know how they fight with them, but I'm sure they favor close combat like the yellow people. We can defeat them the way we defeated the yellow people!"

Trees had become the safest place for the youth. Whenever war broke out, they went up the highest branches to hide. The prolonged wars had forced them to become as comfortable as monkeys. When Laceng had discovered that the yellow people fought using clubs, preferring to come close to an enemy, he organized the youth to climb trees and ambush the enemy with a rain of arrows. The trick worked. Hundreds of yellow people died in a single morning. The rest fled in disarray. That same night the elders gave up the land they were fighting for and opted to move. A wise decision, for the yellow people would not fall for the same trick twice.

"The giants are not my biggest worry," Laceng said. "It's the jothokwo."

"Jothokwo?" Deyu and Ganzi said in unison. "Those things don't exist!"

"I thought so, too."

"Is that what's in the forest?" Deyu said.

"Yes," Laceng answered, gravely.

When all his followers had crossed the river, he told them about the jothokwo and his plans of defending the land. They were only about four hundred, mostly female. He was uncertain of victory, but he did not let the doubts show when he addressed them.

"It is sad that we have to divide our nation," he said. "We might perish in our stupidity, but we can overcome all these evils and live in this paradise. First, we must prepare to fight the giants. We need thousands of poisoned arrows for that battle. Then I have to find out how to defeat the jothokwo. I will spend the night here with five volunteers. The rest of you must go back up to prepare the arrows. Be nice to your parents. Say goodbye properly."

Deyu cried when she heard this, but at once led a team to pick didonto leaves and purple mushrooms, ingredients of a nonlethal toxicant which they could produce in large quantities over a short period of time. It would paralyze the enemy with instant, severe headache, drowsiness, and a lethargy that lasts for a couple of days. She split the pickers into two, some went to find the leaves and mushrooms while others gathered wood to make arrows.

Just before sunset the Circle of Elders announced that they would march the next day, with or without their children, with or without their prophesied saviour. The rebel youth moved away from the main camp in order to continue making battle preparations without the interference of the elders. Many did not say goodbye to their parents.

Ganzi, Deyu, and four others volunteered to stay with Laceng down in the valley. Deyu was avoiding her mother. She feared staying in the camp would soften her heart. She was the only woman who stayed in the forest that night, and it turned out to be a very long night. They hid up in the trees, for legend had it that the jothokwo had stiff joints and could not climb, which would explain why they had not gone up the steep, zigzag path in the plateau wall. The moon rose early and shrouded the valley with its beauty. A fresh breeze blew from the mountains, stirring the scent of flowers, encouraging crickets to sing love ballads. Frogs in the river drummed up a wedding melody in unison to the wild dogs that barked at the moon from beyond the horizon. Laceng thought about Deyu, about the gap between her front teeth, the braids that dangled over her ears, about her long legs and her pointed breasts. He wished they could dance in the beauty of this full moon.

He knew the jothokwo were coming when the crickets suddenly fell silent. Frogs plopped into the river and vanished to the bottom. The dogs stopped their racket. The breeze died out. The scent of flowers evaporated. The stench of rot filled the night with a suffocating aura. A dark cloud swept over the face of the moon, bringing a heavy darkness upon paradise.

"Get ready," Laceng whispered at the same time that Ganzi said, "They are here."

Laceng peered into the darkness, searching, waiting to see the green eyes and white teeth. Nothing. They waited. The odor grew stronger and stronger.

"Look," one of the others whispered. Konta. The best hunter Laceng had ever known. He once nearly died under the claws of a lion. He survived, mysteriously. Some say the lion's spirit possessed him. "Across the river!"

Laceng peered through the foliage. He saw the reflection of green eyes and white teeth in the water. The clouds parted, and though the moon did not come out again, enough light fell down to illuminate the jothokwo. Dozens of creatures shuffled on the narrow piece of land between the river and the plateau wall, walking in a single file, eyes turned skywards, knowing there was food up there, far out of reach. They hooted, producing a sound too low for those at the top of the plateau to hear. It filled Laceng with terror. It made him think of an owl prophesying a death. He and his men were so taken up with the creatures at the riverside that they did not notice they were besieged until a hoot came from below. Scores of dead creatures had gathered under their trees. Hands stretched out trying to grab them. Pieces of flesh clung to their bones like rags. Their eyes were like green flames. Blackish liquid like thick and gooey saliva drooled from their mouths.

He and his men were so taken up with the creatures at the riverside that they did not notice they were besieged until a hoot came from below. Scores of dead creatures had gathered under their trees. Hands stretched out trying to grab them. Pieces of flesh clung to their bones like rags. Their eyes were like green flames. Blackish liquid like thick, gooey saliva drooled from their mouths.

Somebody screamed, lost his grip on the branch, and fell. Laceng thought it was Pangana. He fell right into the hands of the jothokwo. He did not touch the ground. They held him up in the air and took him away. His screams were so loud that Laceng was sure the people in the camp could hear.

Laceng shot an arrow and struck one of the creatures carrying Pangana right in the head. The creature fell to the ground. Ganzi and the others fired, too, hitting the creatures' heads. The ghouls were so many that the moment one fell another took its place. Pangana grabbed a low-hanging branch and hauled himself away from the dead things, but one had a firm grip on his leg. Its fingers dug deep into his flesh, spewing blood.

Laceng shot an arrow into its eye socket. Still, it did not let go. Soon several other hands were digging into the leg. Pangana kicked and struggled. Arrows hit the jothokwo. For a moment Laceng thought they were winning. These were not supernatural creatures after all. Arrows could knock them out.

Then one ghoul, as tall and big as the giants, pushed its way into view. Its hands could reach the branch on which Pangana held on for dear life. Laceng shot it. As it went down, another giant took its place. This one managed to grab hold of Pangana's waist. Two arrows struck its head. It fell, but its claws had sunk deep into Pangana and tore him off the tree. He vanished in the sea of rotting bodies. His screams stopped suddenly. The ensuing silence confirmed his death.

Laceng and his men stopped shooting. They watched the dead things feasting, heard the sickening sound of sucking and munching and growling. It might have been a pack of dogs fighting for a kill. Laceng felt something wet and cold roll down his face, something like a worm. He did not slap it away for he knew that he was crying.

Tears blurred his vision. When one corpse that an arrow had knocked out rose back to its feet, he thought his eyes were playing tricks on him. The creature swayed as though drunk. It hooted at the dark sky and plucked the arrow out of its skull. A chunk of flesh was stuck on the arrowhead. It looked at the arrow, threw it away, and dived in to fight for the food. One by one, the fallen jothokwo staggered back to their feet, plucked out the arrows, and joined the feast.

Laceng screamed in rage, in helplessness, in frustration. He berated himself for disobeying his elders, for not listening to the wise, old Gutu. His rashness had led to the death of a fine young man, and it might kill the remaining five.

The ghouls finished eating up Pangana. They stood underneath the trees, their fingers stretched out, their teeth bared, hooting, as though praying to demons to send them another meal. Laceng feared that one of his people would get tired, slip off, and fall into the rotting hands of the ghouls. He prayed to his ancestors, to the gods who sent the sign on the day that he was born. He begged for protection. He closed his eyes. He could no longer bear to see the green eyes, or the teeth, or the bits of flesh that hung to the dead bones like rags. But he could not shut out the hooting. It grew louder and louder as more ghouls gathered underneath until he could no longer hear his own thoughts.

Until he could no longer hear anything, not even the hoots.

At first, he thought he had gone deaf. Soon he regained his sense of smell. The flowers emitted a sweet perfume that made him drowsy. Little by little, sounds returned to paradise—the crickets, the frogs, the crow of wild roosters, the birds. Dawn was approaching. The ghouls had fled the rise of daylight. Laceng and his men had survived.

"They are gone," he said.

He got no response from the others. For a brief moment he feared they were all dead and he was the sole survivor.

"I can smell again," Ganzi said.

Someone chuckled. Laceng did not know who, but he did not berate him. It was the laughter of relief. He would have laughed out, too, but Pangana's death filled him with guilt.

Though the dead things were gone and life had returned to paradise, they did not climb down from the trees until the cold light of dawn filled the world. There was no dew that morning. They stood around Pangana's corpse, staring at it in silence and horror. The back of his head was missing, had been chewed off. The skull was empty, licked clean of brain. The rest of the body did not have any bite marks.

"He died because of my foolishness," Laceng said.

Nobody replied. He thought about what he would tell Pangana's mother, a little old woman who had lost all her children to war. This was a death they could have avoided. He thought about what he would tell the elders, how he would apologize, what punishment they would give him.

"I have failed you," he said.

"Are we giving up?" Ganzi asked.

"I do not know how to fight things that cannot die."

Ganzi picked up an arrow. It still had rotting flesh attached to it.

"This is wood and bone," he said, waving the arrow about. "It has no magic, not even poison, but it knocked them out. Do you know what it means? It did not kill them, but it knocked them out. Can you see what I'm seeing?"

Maggots crawled down the shaft toward Ganzi's hand. The supernatural jothokwo did not remain standing when the arrows hit them. They fell. They were knocked out for several moments. Did that not mean that ordinary weapons could kill them?

Just then the first rays of the rising sun fell upon the piece of flesh stuck to the arrowhead. The flesh sizzled. Smoke erupted so suddenly that Ganzi threw away the arrow in fright. It fell on Pangana's corpse. The flesh continued to smolder until it turned into black ash. Laceng picked up another arrow and shoved it into the sunlight. The flesh burst into smoke with a sizzle. Within a few heartbeats it was reduced to black ash. Sunlight was the answer, but how could they take it into the night?

"This is the proof," Deyu said. "Proof that you were born to lead us to this valley. The only thing stopping us from settling here is a creature that dies upon contact with your father, the sun. You cannot give up, not after seeing this proof."

*What about the giants*, Laceng wanted to say, but he kept his mouth shut, for the other young men had the same expression on their faces as what he saw on Deyu's and Ganzi's. They would not let him walk away. They believed in him. He had to defeat the giants and the ghouls and give them a home.

A shout from the river interrupted the moment. They turned to see a column of people descending the plateau wall. Gutu was on a raft, rowing fast as though in pursuit of Deyu's mother, who was already halfway through the water, swimming frantically, shouting his name. Deyu took his hand, and hid behind him, as if to use him as a shield against her mother.

"You are alive," her mother said, scrambling out of the water. "We heard the screams. We thought you were all dead."

"We are alive," Deyu said.

Gutu's raft landed very close to them. The medicine man stepped onto the banks. His little feet sunk in the mud. He stared at Laceng for a long time, as though wondering what he was. Laceng did not know what to make of the stare. Deyu clasped his hands tight in support.

"Who died?" Gutu finally said.

"Pangana," Laceng said.

He wondered why Gutu had descended into paradise. He did not have to make the trip to get information. Another silence between them followed, stressed by the splashes of swimmers, the landing of rafts, the voices asking a hundred questions.

"We survived them," Laceng said. "We can defeat them with your support. Don't go."

Gutu gave him a faint smile. "Some families have already started the move," he said. "By the middle of the day, the camp will be empty. Just so you know, after hearing the screams, many of the young people who had chosen to stay have now decided to move. If you want, you can come with us. If you insist on staying, please receive our blessings. If you change your mind after we have gone, follow us. We shall travel with the setting sun to our right."

Gutu suggested that they bury Pangana immediately because of the nature of his death. They dug a hole by the banks and put him in with charms to guide him in the other world since his life had ended before he was ready to go. When done with the rituals, Gutu got onto his raft.

"We go," he said to Deyu's mother.

She shook her head, a little sadly. "I've lost all my

children," she said, in a soft voice that stunned the youth. "I don't want to lose the only one left. If she is to die here, let me die with her."

Gutu gave a slight nod and took his raft back to the other bank. As Laceng watched him climb the wall, he wondered if they would ever see each other again.

By noon of that day, the remnants of the nation gathered to deliberate their options. They were about five hundred people, mostly youth, many female, and a few adults like Deyu's mother who did not wish to part with their children. Some were too sick, or too old, to travel.

"We will have thousands of poison arrows ready by morning," Deyu said.

"Then we'll take to the trees," Laceng said. "We position ourselves in an egg formation. We lure the giants into the egg and hope the ambush wipes them out."

He did not sound convincing. His voice was tired. He still had no idea how to defeat the jothokwo. Weariness poured out of his skin like sweat. The long night without sleep had given him a slight headache. But his followers gave a huge roar of self-motivation.

"We could make fire arrows," Deyu said.

"Fire what?"

"The jothokwo flesh burns into ashes upon contact with the sun."

"Yes?"

"And the sun is merely a huge ball of fire in the sky."

"How shall we take the sun into the night?"

"What are fire arrows?" Ganzi asked.

"I don't know," Deyu said. "But it's what will defeat the jothokwo."

For the first time since he started the rebellion, Laceng smiled. He hugged her so tightly that she gasped in pain. He knew the look she had, the slight frown that creased her brows, the way her lips curved downwards, and he could feel something cooking in her head.

The next morning, shortly after sunrise, they went

down the plateau to ambush the giants. Fresh energy surged in Laceng's limbs. He bounded over the undergrowth like an antelope. He felt as though he were flying.

They climbed high branches to gain maximum advantage to make it harder for the giants to get at them. They wore a camouflage of leaves. The enemy would have to look very hard to spot them. Five men, the fastest runners, stayed on the ground to bait the behemoths.

They waited.

The Kalaba came as the sun reached the middle of the sky. The shadows were short. The flowers had folded into themselves to escape the heat and did not emit their perfumes. Laceng had dozed off. He did not know how long he was asleep. Drums woke him up. For several heartbeats he could not tell what was happening.

"They are here!" Ganzi said.

The giants were singing, drumming, and chanting, creating an atmosphere to intimidate. It seemed to take forever before Laceng heard his five men running very fast through the egg. As planned, they had attacked the giants, killed a few, and fled. The enemy took the bait and pursued. Right into the trap.

There were hundreds of giants. Laceng waited at the thin end of the egg, nearest the river. The first giant, their leader, who wore a leopard skin and had a goat horn hairstyle, came charging out of the undergrowth, holding his knife high as he roared. Laceng's arrow hit his chest. The giant fell without knowing what killed him.

Ganzi blew a horn, which shrilled amidst the music of the behemoths. At once, a storm of arrows poured down. Scores of the giants fell within a few heartbeats, many dead, others writhing in agony at the sudden attack of severe headache.

The giants were stunned. Their music stopped. They shouted and ran around in confusion, very much like the yellow people. They had expected to fight face to face, not with unseen enemies hidden up trees. But the Kalaba were better warriors than the yellow people. Soon after the shock of the ambush had waned, they reorganized themselves.

A lone drum started to beat. The drummer must have been out of reach of the arrows, for Laceng had instructed his people to aim at the leaders and musicians. Eliminating these weakened the morale of the attacking force. The giants retreated.

Laceng jumped from branch to branch, shooting the fleeing giants, hitting his targets with great accuracy. His people pursued, jumping from tree to tree, nimble as monkeys. A few lost their footing and fell. The giants cut them to pieces before they hit the ground. Nearly half of the giants escaped and vanished safely out of arrow range. They left their wounded in the grass, paralyzed with poison, unable to flee.

For a moment he thought they had won. But then they heard confusing sounds coming from the distance.

*Thonk! Thonk! Thonk!*

Axes cutting wood.

Laceng ordered his fighters to remain alert up in the trees. For a long time the sounds of lumbering filled the world.

When the enemy reappeared, they had large shields, each of which protected about six men. Some had papyrus mats. While these were not as effective, it made it harder for the arrows to find targets.

The giants had also armed themselves with rocks, which they threw into the trees. Some missiles hit their targets and sent Laceng's fighters tumbling off their high places to be cut to pieces as they fell. But the young warriors had very effective camouflage. The giants could not easily spot them. Each time the goliaths stepped out from behind their shields to search the trees, arrows ripped into their flesh and poison seeped into their blood, turning even simple flesh wounds into crippling blows. It was a battle of wits, of patience, of subterfuge. It raged for a long time.

As the sun started to slide into its bed, the giants beat

the retreat drums, afraid of darkness finding them near the forest. They took with them as many of their wounded as they could, but they left behind scores who were unable to walk because the poison turned their legs into water.

Laceng's fighters came down from the trees. Sixteen were dead. Compared to the hundreds of giants who lay amidst the flowers, it was a great victory. The smell of blood overpowered the sweet perfume. The wounded giants surrendered, their faces twisted in agony, their limbs swollen with paralysis.

"Take us to safety," one of the giants said, using gestures, signs, and drawings in the blood-soaked ground. "We are at your mercy. The jothokwo don't eat brains of the dead. They only eat the living. After one day those they eat turn into jothokwo. Save us from that fate."

The horror showed on Laceng's face as he eyed the diagrams in the mud. He was thinking about Pangana, who would return to them, not as a friend, but as an evil creature with green eyes and white teeth.

He looked toward the sky. The scorching kiss of noontime was gone. A warm glow caressed his exhausted skin. The shadows were growing longer. Soon the sun would turn red and sink out of sight, plunging the world into darkness, luring the jothokwo out of the forest. Laceng looked at the scores of wounded men. The ghouls would have a big feast, and the next day their numbers would increase by hundreds of giants.

"Is there an antidote to this poison?" he asked Ganzi.

"Gutu knows," Ganzi said. "But he isn't here, and we need to carry away these beasts before darkness falls."

"Carry them to where? Up the plateau? They are so heavy, and we are so tired that darkness will fall before we have moved half of them."

"What about the town?" Ganzi said. "The wall is not complete. But look at all these shields. They can fill the gaps in the fence. If the ghouls cannot climb trees, then surely they can't climb a wall."

The shields were flat and twice the length of a man. Using these as stretcher-sleighs, Laceng's warriors dragged the captured giants to the compound. When Deyu and the others saw Laceng return in victory, they ululated, sang songs, and beat drums. They poured down from the plateau to help drag the wounded off the battlefield.

"The fire arrows," Laceng said to Deyu as she gave him a big hug.

"We made a thousand," she said, her face glowing with pride at his victory. "Look," she showed him her palms and fingers. They were calloused from sharpening sticks and shaping arrows. "We soaked them in odino oil."

"But how do they work?"

She took him to the riverbank where they had piled the arrows. She lit a fire by rubbing soft henirot wood against a rock. She then set an arrow aflame and gave it to him. He shot the arrow into the trunk of the nearest tree. It stuck. The fire burned for a long time. The arrow eventually turned to ash, and all that remained was a black spot marking the trunk.

"Good work, my queen," he said. "We shall need all the odino oil you have."

"You don't need more," she said. "These arrows are already soaked."

"We do," he said. "To create a wall of fire outside the incomplete wall."

:::

Thick darkness lay upon the land by the time they had brought in all the wounded prisoners and finished setting up their defenses. Deyu poured the remaining oil onto a pile of firewood ringed around the wall. Rather than leave the prisoners alone in the town, Laceng and his fighters stayed to protect them. They wanted to test their weapons on the jothokwo. Most of the others went back up the plateau. Though he was against it, Deyu stayed.

"Take a rest," she said. "Eat food. We have a long night ahead."

Laceng did not realize how exhausted he was until he sat down on a mat. He dozed off as he ate the meal she had prepared—roast chicken and millet bread. She woke him up several times to finish the food. After he had eaten she let him sleep. Almost as soon as he started to dream, silence fell upon paradise. The frogs stopped croaking, the crickets stopped singing, the wind stopped blowing, and the flowers could not emit their sweet perfumes. A suffocating stench choked the night.

He woke up.

The compound was abuzz with panic. Fighters ran about, taking up positions atop ladders on the fence. They stuck torches on the wall and waited. They lit the firewood ringed around the wall. The flames leapt high, lighting the world with the redness of hope. Laceng, perched on a ladder, looked beyond the flames into the darkness. The flowers had folded up their petals, as though trying to recoil into buds to hide from the approaching terror. The low hooting came out of the darkness long before the jothokwo appeared. Laceng thought he was ready until he saw the first ghoul.

"Pangana!" someone screamed, and fell off the ladder.

Laceng watched his dead friend limping out of the darkness. His legs seemed to have no joints, the death wound gaping on his head. He was not rotting like the rest. He only looked dirty. Mud clung to his body. His eyes blazed like a green fire, his teeth bared, shining brighter than anything Laceng had ever seen. His hands were stretched out, as though his senses of sight and smell were now in his palms, leading him to what would have been his home.

Several other people jumped off the ladders and cowered in the darkness below, amidst the wounded giants. Laceng took out an arrow, torched it, and armed his bow; but his hands were shaking so much that his shot was wide of the mark. Pangana shuffled on, taking no notice of the arrow that fell somewhere behind him or the flames in front of him. He walked with hungry determination. Behind him, hundreds of green eyes glowed in the darkness, thousands of white teeth shone like fireflies. The hooting came like a breeze of foul air.

Terror gripped Laceng. What if the fire did not destroy the fiend?

He watched Pangana get closer to the flames as though the fire did not exist, watched him step onto the burning wood. For several moments it looked as though he would walk right through the fire. Then he let out a long hoot. It sounded like a horn being blown out of tune. His body burst into flames. He tried to beat it off, but he fell to the ground. His head leapt off his burning body and rolled into the darkness.

Other jothokwo stopped. They were now close enough to the flames to feel the heat. They had seen what had happened to their newest member and were suddenly afraid of the fire.

Laceng's palms were sweaty. He took out another arrow. It felt slimy. He torched it, loaded it, and shot at the stationary ghouls. It took an eternity as it sped through the night. It struck a ghoul right in the chest. The thing fell. Its friends looked at it in dull curiosity. For a moment the arrow stood in the chest, a thin flame dancing. Laceng thought the fire would never catch. Then abruptly the ghoul burst into flames. It hooted in pain and tried to beat out the fire. Its friends could not give any help. It turned into ash faster than Pangana had. Its head also rolled away into the darkness.

In the next moment fire arrows poured down upon the jothokwo. The fighters who had fled now scrambled back up the ladders to join the massacre. The living dead did not flee. They poured forward, their hunger driving them to attempt to cross the wall of fire. They were so many that Laceng's arrows could not stop them. They beat the flames with shrubs. In some places they succeeded in creating a gap in the fire for them to walk through. Fire arrows rained upon them. The wood soaked in odino oil again burst into flames, closing the gap.

Eventually, the jothokwo realized the futility of their efforts. They retreated into the darkness, out of reach of the arrows. Laceng could see their green eyes and white teeth shining with hunger. He thought they were waiting for the fire to burn itself out.

"We should pursue them," he told Ganzi.

"Are you mad?" Ganzi said.

"Our fire does not have enough fuel to burn all night. Let's chase them away."

The smell of victory filled Laceng with pride and tremendous courage. He scurried down the ladder, urging his fighters to go on the offensive. They went through the gates, torches blazing in one hand, bows in the other. They created a gap in the fire wall and went out into the territory of the dead. The jothokwo rushed at them, but the fire arrows felled them, turning them into ashes.

Laceng saw something roll about in the grass. He turned his torch to it and saw a bodiless head. It was still alive, the hair singed, flesh charred, teeth shining white in the blackened skull, eyes bubbling with green froth. The head snapped at him. Its teeth smashed into each other like the clash of two rocks. He jumped back. Before he could warn anyone else, the head leapt and sunk its teeth into a man's calf. The man screamed and fell. The head then sunk its teeth into his skull and tore off a huge piece in one bite. Its tongue snaked out and licked the brains. The slapping sucking gurgling seemed to be the only sound in the world.

"Heads!" Laceng screamed in panic. "The heads are not dead!"

His warning was a heartbeat too late. Screams erupted all around him as more heads found victims. Laceng speared the first one with the torch. The stick went right through an eye, splashing green goo all over, and pinned the head to the ground. The flame went out. It snarled and glared at him with the remaining eye. Brains drooled out of the corners of its mouth. It jumped at him, wrenching the torch off the ground, but he jumped away from its teeth.

"Retreat!" he screamed, needlessly. His fighters were already scrambling back to the safety behind the wall. Hundreds of heads chased them. They jumped over the flames. Some peopled were burned, but they scrambled back through the gate.

The heads rolled over the fire, which could not harm them, and three jumped through the gate before it could close. One of these found a woman's legs, and it was sucking her brains out when Laceng recovered from the shock. He picked a rock and smashed the head. Goo splashed his feet. His fighters smashed the other two heads. Still, the things did not die. The teeth kept clattering on the ground. Some flew into the air and sunk into living flesh, but since they were detached from the jaws, the teeth were no more irksome than thorns.

The heads threw themselves against the wall, looking for a way in until they found a weak point, the gaps that Laceng's men had hurriedly filled earlier that night. One shield was not firm in the ground. It tottered and collapsed against bumping from the heads. Luckily, someone saw the danger, and several men ran to hold it up. The heads sensed the weak point and gathered in large numbers. Laceng's fighters threw heavy objects over the wall and squashed several heads, but that did not diminish the threat. The heads threw themselves at the wall in rapid succession, smashing against the shield with the force of a huge rock.

The ring of fire died out. The jothokwo came out again. This time their sheer numbers prevailed over the deluge of arrows. They reached the wall. They found another weak spot and ripped off a shield. Laceng's fighters concentrated their fire arrows on the spot, desperate to stop the ghouls from getting in. While the dead creatures burst into flames, their heads ran riot in the compound. His people climbed the ladders for safety, but the prisoners on the ground provided the ghouls with a feast.

Laceng jumped down, picked up a club, and went on a smashing rampage. It was easy to spot the heads from their green eyes and white teeth. Ganzi and a dozen others joined in the smashing campaign while the rest of them stayed up on ladders and in the trees, keeping the bodied ghouls outside the walls.

The night was longer than the previous one. Laceng thought it would never end. Finally, as dawn approached, the onslaught relented. The timing mechanisms in the jothokwo set off alarms. They retreated to the forest to escape the rising sun.

Unlike the previous night, the frogs did not start to croak, nor did the crickets start singing upon the departure of the living dead. The breeze did not blow. The flowers did not unfurl to emit their sweet perfumes.

Worried, Laceng looked out over the fence. He could not see the green eyes and white teeth in the darkness. That did not allay his fears. The foul smell remained in the air. The dead were still in the vicinity. They had not retreated into the forest.

The sun came up. The odor stayed in the air. The perfume of flowers did not grace the morning. Exhausted, puzzled, cautious, Laceng crept out of the compound, his soldiers behind him, carrying torches and fire arrows, though these were unnecessary in the sun. They followed the smell. Before long they found the first group of heads cowering in a grove of trees by the riverside. The heads were unable to roll back to the forest in time and hid wherever they found thick vegetation to offer them protection from the sun. Using long sticks, his soldiers pushed them into the sun's rays and vaporized every single one of them.

At last the flowers burst open, blossoming afresh. The birds crept out of their nests and sang belatedly to welcome the new day. Laceng fell on his knees and thanked his ancestors. The worst was over. They would make paradise their home. The only threat left was the giants. If they attacked again, they would wipe out his people. They certainly would have found an antidote to the poison, and the ambush trick could not work twice on the same people.

When he got back to the compound, the effects of the poison had worn off the remaining prisoners. They had regained the strength to walk on their own. About thirty of them had fallen prey to the jothokwo. The remaining hundred had something in their eyes that Laceng, in his exhaustion, did not recognize.

They bowed low, speaking rapidly in their language. Though he did not understand their speech, he knew they thought he was a god. He, after all, had defeated the undead.

He released them. He drew diagrams on the ground to indicate peace between his people and theirs. The giants bowed and ran back to the mountains.

:::

Later that day the behemoths returned, but not to fight. They brought a lot of gifts with them. Their king came, too. He wore a robe of lion skin. His hair was styled to resemble a multitude of goat horns. He went down on his knees and bowed low to indicate his submission to the rule of Laceng. Using signs, diagrams, and a little speech, for they had by now discovered that their languages shared certain words, they promised to live in peace with one another. The King gave up all claims to the valley of colour and sweet smells. His people would remain up in the mountains. By defeating the jothokwo, Laceng was the rightful owner of paradise.

That next day Laceng sent five of the fastest men to go after the rest of the Jolabong, who were migrating with the sun to their left. Five days later the Jolabong returned. Parents reunited with their brave children. They sang and celebrated long into the night. Gutu asked Laceng to forgive him for his mistake. The Circles of Elders crowned Laceng king. In the history of the nation, he was the first man to rule them before getting married, when he was barely out of his childhood.

For nearly a whole moon after the first victory, Laceng and his men battled the jothokwo. They never lost another person again to the dead creatures. They burnt them by the masses every night. They would set traps, and the living dead would walk into a pile of firewood. When a great number were in the middle, Laceng would shoot fire arrows and set them all ablaze. After sunrise they would destroy the heads.

Gradually, the jothokwo numbers reduced. Encouraged, Laceng and his men invaded the forest. They found the nest of the dead, which was a large cave in the depths of the jungle, and set the last creatures on fire. Finally, life returned to the jungle. Flowers spread into the wood and lit up the darkness with beauty.

About six moons after they finally settled in their new home, Laceng married Deyu. It was the most lavish wedding the nation had ever known. The Kalaba came down from the mountains with many gifts. The two nations celebrated together, rejoicing over the end of evil and the beginning of the reign of the Son of the Sun.

And that, my dear children, is why we are called Jolaceng.

## ::: About the Author :::

Dilman Dila is a writer, filmmaker, all round storyteller, and author of a critically acclaimed collection of short stories, *A Killing in the Sun*. He has been shortlisted for the Commonwealth Short Story Prize (2013) and for the Nommo Awards for Best Novella (2017), and long listed for the BBC International Radio Playwriting Competition (2014), among many accolades. His short fiction have featured in several anthologies, including *African Monsters, Myriad Lands, AfroSF v2*, and the *Apex Book of World SF 4*. His digital art has been on exhibition in USA and Uganda, and his films include the masterpiece *What Happened in Room 13* (2007), and *The Felistas Fable* (2013), which was nominated for Best First Feature by a Director at AMAA (2014) and winner of four major awards at Uganda Film Festival (2014). You can watch and support his short films on patreon.com/dilstories and you can find more on his life and works on his website dilmandila.com.

# ::: **Publication History** :::

"Monwor" was first published in *African Monsters: Volume 2* (Fox Spirit Books of Monsters)", Fox Spirit Books, 2015

"Kifaro" was first published in *Weirdbook Annual: Special Zombie Issue* by Wildside Press LLC. 2021

"The Last Storyteller" was first published in *Afrofuturism*, Heady Mix Limited, 2020

"The Flying Man of Stone" was first published in *AfroSF v2*, A Story Time Publication 2015

"Where Rivers Go to Die" was first published in *Redemption Song and Other Stories: The Caine Prize for African Writing 2018*, by The Cain Prize, 2018

"The Green Men Who Fly" was first published in *Unconventional Fantasay Vol 2*, Baltimore Washington Area Worldcon Association, Inc. 2014

"The Terminal Move" was first published by Fox & Raven Publishing (October 16, 2013), reprinted in *Ravensmoot: An Anthology of Speculative Fiction*, Fox & Raven Publishing (December 16, 2013)